MARVEL® COMICS

GENERATION X

Scott Lobdell & Elliot S! Maggin

ILLUSTRATIONS BY
TOM GRUMMETT & DOUG HAZLEWOOD

Generation X created by
SCOTT LOBDELL & CHRIS BACHALO

MARVEL COMICS

BYRON PREISS MULTIMEDIA COMPANY, INC.

NEW YORK

BOULEVARD BOOKS, NEW YORK

Special thanks to Ginjer Buchanan, Steve Roman, Stacy Gittelman, Mike Thomas, Steve Behling, and John Conroy.

GENERATION X

A Boulevard Book
A Byron Preiss Multimedia Company, Inc. Book

PRINTING HISTORY
Boulevard paperback edition / June 1997

The Putnam Berkley World Wide Web site address is
http://www.berkley.com

Check out the Byron Preiss Multimedia Co., Inc. site on the
World Wide Web: http://www.byronpreiss.com

Make sure to check out *PB Plug*, the science fiction/fantasy newsletter, at
http://www.pbplug.com

ISBN 1-57297-223-8

BOULEVARD
Boulevard Books are published by The Berkley Publishing Group,
200 Madison Avenue, New York, New York 10016.
BOULEVARD and its logo
are trademarks belonging to Berkley Publishing Corporation.

PRINTED IN THE UNITED STATES OF AMERICA

10 9 8 7 6 5 4 3 2 1

To Ike—the best friend a son could ever have.

—SL

To my students, over the years.
Get in touch, would you?

—ES!M

GENERATION X ®

CHAPTER ONE
BIOSPHERE

The pine forest to the north of Snow Valley, Massachusetts, near Stockbridge, is a little blank smudge on the road maps. There is no road. The only distinguishing feature is the snaky path that the Mad River takes down Sugar Mountain, eventually to join the Housatonic River, and wash into the Atlantic. Only the property map sketched out at the home of Edna Gross, the County Registrar of Deeds in Lenox, tells what really occupies that smudge of Mad River Valley at the base of Sugar Mountain, somewhere between the boyhood home of singer James Taylor and the old art studio of the legendary illustrator Norman Rockwell: a large irregular tract of acreage to either side of the river, once belonging to a prestigious private school, now owned and operated by the Xavier Institute for Higher Learning.

Rockwell was the visual scribe of rural New England, the place where America takes place. He made a great deal of the people he found here. The artist chronicled, through the faces he rendered on the covers of *Collier's* and the *Saturday Evening Post*, what the American nation was becoming through the folk of these little towns. One has to wonder what he would have made of Jonothon Starsmore.

Jonothon really had no face to speak of. More accurately, he had about half a face. A top half. The bottom half was a free-floating suspension of plasma waves, matter in the process of converting to pure energy, over which Jono had only nominal control. That was what he needed to change at Xavier's School for Gifted Youngsters.

Jono had been a cute kid. He shined back in the old country, like a jewel. Like pretty much all the *homo superior* kids until they start manifesting their special abilities. On weekends in Glasgow in the little towns in western Scotland, he had been a promising young rock musician, swooned over and chased around through basement clubs and the odd hotel hallway until his voice box started to turn into pure energy.

It started for Jonothon Starsmore when he was an eleven-year-old Glasgow schoolboy. He casually blasted a noisy political sound truck out of existence with a burst of energy from his midsection. The blast left a pinhole of roiling psionic power that doctors who didn't know any better mistook for a birthmark until they looked closer.

Gradually, Jonothon had occasion to do away with increasingly large chunks of the matter that composed his body. There was the rescue of the old lady who was tumbling onto the tram track. Then the young woman on that bridge by the Firth of Clyde being chased by those toffs whose brass knuckles fused to their teeth as they chewed their fists in pain. That one was the first time he got the idea that he could use this power surgically: he could pull back on it, limit it through force of will. But that little maneuver cost Jono what was left of his stomach cavity. No one would ever accuse Jono of being a cute kid again.

Just a few years ago, Jono scared some of his

classmates by undoing his bandages to reveal the white-hot plasma suspension of his former body from thighs to sternum. This prompted the local authorities to encourage his parents into putting together a home schooling program for which they were ill qualified and less inclined. So for a few months Jonothon's math teacher was his father who still ran his dry cleaning shop out of an old NCR cash register. He took French with his mother, also a condition of dubious benefit. Jono once walked with his mom into a little restaurant in Normandie, both of them excited to try out their French on someone who didn't speak anything else. When Mum said a simple burr-infested "Oui" in answer to the hostess's question, "Deux pour petit-déjeuner?" the hostess's cute smile darkened and she turned, saying in English, "Oh, right this way."

Uncle Ian the auto mechanic, though, sure did know his physics. Ian and Jono figured out the proper oil-to-air ratio in Master Tomas's old beater of a '55 Mercedes using an ohm-meter, checking the results against an oscilloscope. Pretty soon they measured the side-particle throw-weight in photons through the micro-pores in the bandages over Jono's chest. They found that if Jono could harness the waste material of his personal bio-generator alone, he could focus enough power to lift downtown Glasgow to Saturn and back between lunch and dinner. It was Uncle Ian's physics classes that prompted Jono to take seriously the possibility of enrolling at Xavier's School.

Now here he was in America not a year later, climbing up the geodesic grid on the inside of the biosphere to spy on Emma Frost, the headmistress, and Monet St. Croix, one of Jono's fellow students. Jonothon could not imagine that either Emma or Monet could be unaware of him there—particularly given that Emma was a powerful telepath; very little got by her—but they were both too busy to notice. So he watched as they worked out their combat maneuvers. Monet, who was some kind of Algerian princess according to what little she let on, flexed somehow, in that ineffable, more-than-human way, all over her body when she launched herself into flight. Like Hideo Nomo about to launch a pitch, only hotter.

Emma was the White Queen, the mutant telepath who once trained a group of mutant kids called the Hellions. They were all gone now. Squashed like bugs by some super-powered doofus named Fitzroy, but Jono knew what'd really gotten the Hellions: government. Not like the government in Washington or London. All governments. Everywhere. The collective hive mind of people that set themselves up with great ceremony and ritual and derive their respectability from identifying with those who win a war or step on a problem or perpetuate a delusion. Government got the Hellions and Jono had come here to throw in with other people like himself—or enough like himself—so government would have a harder time and take longer to get him.

Outside, winter was cracking open at the edges. Here in the biosphere, a pair of stupefyingly beautiful super-powered women wove in and out among the treetops of the indoor jungle stalking one another like enemy predators. The game was simple: Monet hunted Emma and Emma hunted Monet. To win, one had to slap the other on her heel.

It was impossible to sneak up on the White Queen. No one sneaks up on a telepath. But Monet had an effective weapon in her speed; she simply had to move faster than either she or Emma could think.

No problem.

The biosphere was a controlled environment in a geodesic dome with the ground space of a football field inside. The various species of vegetation within shouldn't be able to coexist. Tropical herbs from the Amazon basin mixed roots with trillium from the Great White North. An unnaturally fast-growing saguaro from Arizona fought it out for its water supply with a larch from the foothills of the Italian Alps.

Like the school itself, the biosphere was a laboratory. Every time the lavish strains of flora produced what looked to be a mutant strain, Sean Cassidy (aka Banshee, former member of the X-Men), the headmaster, would send out a call over a secret cellular line, and within twenty-four hours Dr. Henry McCoy (aka the Beast, current member of the X-Men and a leading biochemist) would come barreling in to pick apart the little shoot, classify it, and send cuttings to who-knew-where. If it was lucky, the new plant would grow up someday. A lot like the kids here.

Jonothon Starsmore, code-named Chamber—potentially one of the most powerful beings on the planet if only he were to learn how to harness his psionic powers and live until, say, his eighteenth birthday—hung on the struts of the biosphere like a fly on the wall. And if anybody asked why he was here, which they probably wouldn't, he would say that it was to study the training session as Emma drilled Monet. In truth, he just liked to watch the two of them move.

Emma Frost elbowed through the root system of a giant yucca plant to evade detection by Monet. At first glance, Emma seemed to have little in the way of defense against a girl who could fly and lift a mountain and move faster than the image could register on a person's eyes.

Monet flew through the air over the treetops of the biosphere, whipping around in circles. She flew around in an ever-tightening pattern, faster and faster, until the Monet Jono watched was laps behind the one up front.

To Jono, Monet was perfect. Monet was the golden apple under the sun. She spoke the Queen's English with the slightest touch of an accent leftover from a collection of French tutors in Algeria. She grew up as the treasured daughter of a sultan whose tradition generally reserved privileges only for sons. Her skin was golden brown. Her voice was a slow crackling flame. Jono could see how a guy could fall in love with her. He saw it every time she walked among a crowd of people she didn't know to go into a store or wave down a cab or watch a soccer game. Guys fell in love with Monet as the dust settled in her wake, but they lost all illusion of such things when she spoke to them. She was imperious and demanding with every resonation of her being.

Jonothon thought it was odd to see Emma appear uncertain, but in terms of raw power, Monet appeared to outmatch her instructor easily. It was all Emma could do to find a hiding place somewhere in the dirt in the hopes that the girl would trip up, blow her advantage, open herself to attack before she could determine where the White Queen hid.

It didn't seem likely.

As Jono watched, Emma lurked and Monet threw off a humming sound as she vibrated the air. Then, like a skier missing a gate, Monet broke her pattern.

Monet swooped down from the air like a falcon in a power dive. Behind her, the blurred circular image of her spinning path faded like skywriting.

Monet plunged into the earth underneath the yucca tree which Emma rooted around in. As she plowed into the ground, earth sprayed upward. She hardly noticed how far down she dove, so intent was she on finding her teacher's heel.

Then Monet felt a light tap on her own right heel, then her left, just as she submerged into the dirt below the biosphere. Monet was so caught up in the hunt that she had no plan to stop her plunge. Fortunately, the ground broke her descent.

She flapped her arms and she swallowed dirt and she tried to spin but that only bored her in further. She thought about that awful movie about premature burial she'd sneaked a look at as a child. She thought about being in a box below the ground screaming and pulling her hair out and then she thought about being a ghost with nowhere to go except to hang around watching your body decompose and she thought it was going to make her crazy if she didn't stop plowing into the dirt—and then she stopped. Only the two lately insulted heels of her terribly fashionable, antelope-hide super heroine boots jutted out of the ground.

Jono, watching from high on the triangular struts of the inside wall of the dome, scrambled down. Emma, laughing that cruel laugh of hers, got on her knees amidst the yucca root and pulled to no avail on Monet's ankles.

"Is she all right?" Jono projected onto sound waves in the air as he reached the White Queen. He had no mouth, after all, but he had enough psionic energy to simulate pretty much anything—other than his boyish good looks.

"How would I know?"

"Well read her mind or something!"

"Oh I did," Emma offered, "at least enough to know she's healthy. Any deeper into that black hole I don't care to go just now."

"How'd you do that?"

"Do what?"

"Sneak up behind her when she was moving that fast."

"She's fast," the White Queen said, "but not faster than thought. She's an intellectual creature who must sometimes learn to use her instincts."

"Well stand back then," Jono said, and began to

unwrap the bandages over what had once been the lower part of his face.

"Wait a minute, Jono," Emma put a hand on the shoulder of his jacket, which was squishy and shapeless to the touch. There was no flesh to pad him, only free-floating energy. "Are you good enough yet for this kind of surgical gardening?"

"Trust me," Jono said.

The girl's feet waved violently, despite her pinned torso. He shot the first beam of psionic energy at the ground near Monet's head—as thin as a round of psionic energy gets. It chewed up the earth and left a big gully alongside Monet and the perimeter of the Yucca root.

Jono was about to loose another blast between Monet and the main body of the root itself when Monet moved. Fingers, then hands, reaching upward awkwardly, surfaced to either side of the girls' boots. Monet yanked back at the surface of the ground—

—and her hands sank again, deep into the ground that Chamber's bolt of energy had softened to make it easier for her to get out.

Jonothon revved up his power again, concentric circles of energy crackling the air around his body, and Monet leapt out of the ground with the sort of desperate alacrity usually reserved for people in the paths of industrial accidents and nuclear shock waves.

"Are you all right?" and Jonothon's veneer of concern was less obvious than his feeling of guilt at his lame attempt at a rescue.

"Do you know what could have happened," Monet

started softly and slowly, inquiring as to Chamber's sanity, "if the heat of your next bolt of energy had gone just a touch out of control?"

"Well—"

"The dirt itself could have fused into silicon and trapped me in there for, for maybe days."

"Well actually, it's only sand that turns to silicon. Sometimes actually to glass. This is mostly loam and silt and it tends—"

"It tends—" Monet realized that her voice had risen to a shrill pitch and so cut herself off. She brushed off the silt and loam that muddied her face—casually, as though she had meant to get dirty—and lowered her voice to an imperious stage whisper. "—to do what?"

Her usually red spandex flying suit was covered in a layer of mud and filth. She looked like the star of a grunge Kabuki play. Little pieces of mud dribbled to the ground as she talked, and Jonothon almost laughed. Nevertheless, he plunged in: "It tends to harden under heat into a kind of concrete and compress in volume. It's a much more brittle material than glass."

"And you know this from . . . what?"

"Experimentation."

"You run around melting different kinds of soil?"

"Well I did, one day. Back in Scotland, when I was walking the moors with the guys in the band."

"Walking the moors? With your band?"

"Well it was Scotland. There were lots of moors around."

"Fusing soil into cement?"

"Well only that once."

Monet nodded a slow, exaggerated nod.

"And this time too, of course," Jono added.

Jonothon was actually shuffling one foot, looking for activity through which to displace his embarrassment. But Monet, dripping with topsoil, was in charge of the conversation anyway. He wondered whether it would keep her up all night if he slipped a pea under her mattress.

He had very little time to wonder before both of them heard Emma yell.

It was not a blood-curdling scream of the sort you might hear from a woman being attacked by a guy with an eyepatch brandishing a particularly nasty-looking piece of cutlery. It was more like the howl you heard from your mother half-a-second after she walked into your room to find one wall papered with the entire 1986 run of Topps baseball cards fastened there with Elmer's glue.

Monet reached Emma first, her sudden speed removing most of the dirt that had caked on her.

Emma had composed herself by the time Monet arrived, and was staring at something that, as far as she knew, did not belong in the biosphere. It was a kind of big hazy red egg hovering over a big horizontal branch of one of the trees. Emma was looking at it intently, with the kind of look you get when you're surprised by the appearance of an old friend.

"Do you see that?" Emma asked, as if making sure that she wasn't imagining it.

BIOSPHERE

"It's some sort of phenomenon," the student told her teacher in that authoritative way she grew back in her father's court in Algeria. Monet jumped toward the manifestation, floating through the air with a hand extended, "Certainly nothing to be alarmed—" and as she touched it, the shape wobbled and fell out of the air.

"Are you ladies all right?" Jono's artificial voice projected from behind a nearby clump of succulent bushes of a type never before found outside the Amazon rain forest. He stepped into view just in time to see Emma and Monet standing over something on the ground that glowed for a moment, and then vanished.

"What was that?" Jono wanted to know.

Monet shrugged. Emma muttered something, turned on her heel and went for the biosphere airlock.

Monet and Jonothon followed Emma. The White Queen had gotten fairly far in front of them, but the trail of shallow footprints in the corn snow led to the main building.

"What *was* that thing?" Jonothon asked Monet on their own way along Emma's path.

"She thought she recognized it," Monet said.

"Recognized it? She's seen it before?"

"No, I believe she recognized a thought pattern from it."

"She told you she thought the glowing egg was a person?"

"Not as such. She just said 'Haroun,' and then you showed up and she left."

"Haroun?"

They came into the big hallway of the old building
that was now their principal classroom. Xavier's School
occupied the grounds that used to belong to the Massachusetts Academy, one of the oldest private schools in
the country. In fact, its existence predated the American
Revolution by fifty years. When Emma was owner and
sole headmistress of the Academy, she trained the Hellions here.

Then Jono remembered something. "Haroun was
Jetstream's name."

"Jetstream? One of the Hellions. The Moroccan
guy."

"I don't know. He was from one of those places. He
could blow hot plasma blasts behind him and shoot himself up through the air. Better not stand underneath him,
though."

"He died, right?"

"Yeah," Jono said, "with the other Hellions." They
both paused. "Happens," Jono said.

"Who died?" asked Angelo, running down the big
curving staircase, a pair of new thermal boots helping to
hold his feet in shape so he didn't trip over them. "You
look like hell," he noticed Monet's dirt-caked face and
clothes, "what happened?"

"You're no Clark Gable yourself, Skin," Monet said,
and he wasn't. Angelo grew epidermal tissue at an
alarming rate and needed more practice at sucking it all
tight around his body so he looked more like a human
and less like a Chinese sharpé. "Did you see Emma?"

"Oh you're a charmer today, M. She went up to Sean's office and he closed the door."

"He closed the door?" Jonothon repeated. The headmaster almost never closed the door.

"So what's all the buzz?" from Angelo as Monet shoved open the hallway door to a bathroom with an elbow that seemed to be fairly dirt-free.

"We saw a glowing egg she thinks was a dead Moroccan," from Monet.

"Well that doesn't sound like you, M, if you don't mind my saying," Jonothon suggested. "Have you got something against Moroccans?"

"I'm Algerian."

"What? Are you guys not getting along these days?"

"Our countries get along fine. Good fences make good neighbors." With that, she slammed the bathroom door in the two boys' faces.

CHAPTER TWO

DIAMONDS IN THE ROUGH

S ean Cassidy's door stayed closed for about half an hour. Paige was the first to join Jono and Angelo's vigil.

"What's the buzz?" the girl with the breakaway body wanted to know.

Paige Guthrie was better known, if she was known at all, as Husk. "With a name like that," she commented once, "I could go on *American Gladiators*," but Sean had given her the name and she was stuck with it.

Paige had the remarkable, if less than attractive, ability to transform her outer layer of skin to pretty much any material that was necessary to withstand whatever potential injury might accost her, and then to peel or crack or melt off that new layer, revealing the good-as-new, peaches-and-cream Paige underneath. Whenever she did this she felt a little tingly and raw for a few hours, but it was nowhere near as bad as a sunburn. Problem was, with a tendency to have the part of your body you greet the world with turning—sometimes spontaneously—into tree bark or manganese or phlegm, it was hell trying to meet guys.

"What did you see?" Paige asked Jono.

"He saw nothing," Angelo popped in because he felt he should, "just some glowing something-or-other on the ground is all."

"Jonothon?"

"I told you," from Angelo again.

"Did I ask you?"

"Oh," Angelo waggled his hands in the air near his

18

head, and the seams of his skin waggled in the opposite direction. "Sorry."

"What did you see, Jono?" Paige asked.

"Matters more what Emma and M saw," he said as Monet finally emerged from the bathroom and joined them.

"Remarkable," Angelo said, looking Monet up and down as she approached.

"What's remarkable, Skin?"

"You."

"This is news to you?" she asked coolly as Paige rolled her eyes.

"Look at you. Chamber here said you were head-to-ankles in the dirt and it was caked all over you like white on rice. Now there's not a trace. How do you do it?"

"I have super-powers. I can scrub really hard."

The door of the headmaster's office opened a crack, and Sean Cassidy stuck his head out.

The first point of Sean's authority was his size. He thought it was his history, but these kids of whom he was in charge were beginning to grow an impressive history of their own. Sean had done things and seen things of which most people were not even capable of dreaming. He had battled villains, both as a member of Interpol and as an X-Man; combatted the forces of an ignorant hostile government; repeatedly helped save the world for those who hated him. He had a larynx that was unmapped by any known medical authority and a voice that he had trained to shatter steel.

He used that voice—in a more benevolent tone—to say, "Monet, would you come in here?"

"Of course, Sean," she said smoothly, and vanished behind the closed door.

Here's the way things go at a normal high school: Something innocuous happens. Mr. Carrington the French teacher comes in with a toupée over his goosegg skull and everybody acts as though he has been wearing it for years. Or Jimmy gives Tiffany his class ring. Or someone puts a graffito on the girls' room wall that says, "Principal Skinner gets high on bananas." And then the rumors grow. The word is that Mr. Carrington's had his head shaved for an imminent brain surgery procedure and that's why he's been mumbling under his breath using French words he's never taught his classes. And suddenly everyone knows that Tiffany's skipping town next semester so she can go to a clinic to give birth to Jimmy's love child. That's the basic dynamic of information in a conventional high school.

At Xavier's School for Gifted Youngsters, it went the same way, only faster.

Jono, Paige, and Angelo hung around the top of the stairs by the door to Sean's office, as Monet and Emma talked with Sean inside about a manifestation in the biosphere. Jubilee—Jubilation Lee, the thirteen-year-old from the San Fernando Valley who actually had more time logged among the organized mutant establishment than her older schoolmates—appeared and wanted to know: "What's the poop, guys?"

"Is that the same as the buzz?" from Chamber.

"Paige is looking for the buzz and you're looking for the poop. What'll it be, lassies?"

"Some big hoo-hah in Sean's inner sanctum, Jube," said Paige. "Looks heavy."

"How heavy? It's not about the new kid, is it?"

"Much heavier than a new kid," from Paige again. "More like crisis with the X-Men down in the city heavy, or that's what it sounds like. There's a new kid?"

"That's the buzz," from Jubilee down below.

"I thought you were looking for poop," from Jono. "Paige was looking for buzz."

"And whatever happened to haps?" Angelo plugged in. "Back in the 'hood we used to look for haps all the time. Now I'm not even sure they still call it the 'hood."

"What's the haps?" Everett asked as he joined the gathering.

Everett was Synch, who could cast an aura of synchronicity that allowed him to get on the physical vibratory wavelength of pretty much anything you can see, hear, touch, smell, or think about. He was like a matter-hacker, able to use his aura like a computer uses a modem to get into the system of objects outside himself and reprogram them at will. A smiley, self-contained black kid from St. Louis about a year or two younger than Jono, he was the one person in the building with the potential to end up more physically powerful than Jono.

"You've been hanging with Angelo too much," Jubilee told him. "Looks like a big emergency brewing in the sanctum. We're probably all going to New York to help the X-Men fight some super-duper bad guy. Maybe a time traveler, think so?''

"Who said anything about time travelers?'' Jono poked in. "There're no time travelers here.''

"Slippery little suckers, huh?'' from Angelo. "Nudging their way in and out of the continuum like it's Swiss cheese. Like to try that someday.''

"You didn't say anything about time travelers,'' Paige asked, "did you Jonothon?''

"No I didn't say anything of the—''

"Don't get your floppy fingers caught in the time machine door, Skin,'' Everett called up to Angelo. "Find yourself in the Middle Ages and your extremities dribbling off aboard the Starship *Enterprise* or something.''

Paige looked Angelo up and down for a moment, at the skin that hung off his body like bobbling icicles from every eave and said, "That'd be a pretty good cure, huh?''

And Angelo put his face in Paige's. "A cure?'' he asked letting his jowls drip down below his shoulders. "So what's the disease?''

Everett liked to call Sean Cassidy's office the "Bill Room'' behind the headmaster's back. He said it looked like a place where Bill Blass installed the technological systems and Bill Gates did the decorating. And behind his student's back, Sean referred to Everett as "Wit.'' Sean had private nicknames for all of his students to go with their public code names, which made intimacy with the headmaster on an intellectual level very confusing.

DIAMONDS IN THE ROUGH

Everett Thomas—Synch—and his buddy Angelo Espinoza—Skin—were "Wit and Wart." Jonothon Starsmore—Chamber—was "Rock 'n Roll" and Jubilation Lee—Jubilee who shot blinding blasts of light from her hands—was "Fireworks." Monet St. Croix—M who could fly and lift a tank—was, of course, "The Princess" and Paige Guthrie—Husk from Kentucky whose rosy face and blonde hair shone like the noonday sun over the American Midwest—was "Cornfield" or sometimes just "Corny." Sean tended to know pretty much everything his students were saying and thinking about him because, after all, Emma Frost was one of the most powerful telepaths on the planet. The kids trusted her, probably more than they should and certainly more than they would have had they known that she told whatever she knew to the headmaster. Sean trusted her too, though he had not always. His nickname for her—which he came up with despite trying not to—was "Hellion." He never used it and he knew she appreciated that. "What happens in your mind against your will," she told him, "happens not out of venality but out of weakness," and he realized this applied to her as much as it did to him. The kids' latest nickname for Banshee was "Windy."

"Did you get any particular feeling from this manifestation?" Sean asked, sweeping away a random pile of three-and-a-half-inch disks so he had room to put his elbows on his desk.

"It was kind of a—" Emma began but Sean interrupted.

"Actually I wonder if I could get M's impressions first." Emma certainly had come to conclusions about the emotional aura surrounding the big glowing egg they had seen in the biosphere, as telepaths do about pretty much everything. Sean wanted Monet's uninfluenced ideas first.

"Feeling?" Monet wanted to know. "How do you mean?"

"Did it seem friendly?"

"No."

"Unfriendly?"

"No, not at all."

"Anything?"

The girl thought for a moment. "Nothing really. It was . . ."

"Was what, Monet?"

"Well, maybe sad."

"Sad. Anything else?"

"No, I don't think so. Look," Monet changed her tone, "I'm not a telepath or anything. How would I get some mental impression or something?"

"We all have intuition, dear," Emma said.

Sean dug a computer keyboard out from under a pile of journals and loose hanging folders and moved a pile of books from in front of his monitor. On top of the pile was a book called *When Dreams and Heroes Died* by Arthur E. Levine, a former college president, who theorized that the whole social breakdown in adolescent education of the past generation is the result of role models falling off their pedestals in a very public way. Levine thought heroes (and potential ones) ought to keep an aura of mystery around them, if not for their own protection, then for that of those who look up to them. In moving the books, Sean lost his page. He called up Monet's file to punch some notes into it when Monet interrupted.

"Are you trying to be indulgent of us, sir? Because we actually saw this thing."

"He knows that," Emma said as Sean said simultaneously, "I know that," and shot her an exasperated look. That happened a lot.

"I'm not being in any way indulgent, Monet," Sean went on. "To the contrary, I'm trying to be as supportive as I can. It's all about teamwork, lass."

"Okay," said M, "I'm sorry, sir. I'm just a little touchy, I suppose."

"Why?"

"Because I'm not in the habit of seeing things."

"I know," from Sean, who also was not, and simultaneously, "I know," from Emma, who was.

He took a breath and said, "So what about your impressions, Emma?"

"I thought of Haroun al-Rashid when I saw it. Jetstream, from the Hellions."

"Lingering feelings of guilt?" Sean tiptoed.

She shot him a glare.

"I'm just asking. Lingering misplaced unjustified feelings of guilt on your part. It could be that, couldn't it?"

She let out a breath, then, "I thought I sensed a little bit of resentment, actually."

"Resentment. On the manifestation's part?"

"Yes, I think so."

"You think so. Could that be on your part?"

"No," she snapped. Then Emma thought a moment and said, "Actually, yes. It could. Quite the psychologist all of a sudden, Banshee."

Sean motioned to some of the books and journals and reports on the shelves and the desk and the chairs and the cabinets and the floor. "I've been reading up."

Then they heard a noise from outside the door.

"What do you mean I've got no self-control?" Paige got even closer into Angelo's face. She had gotten quite good at this gang-war style of interpersonal negotiation since enrolling here.

"I mean you can't keep from dissing a man for his looks and you can't even figure what you're gonna turn into when you shed your skin."

"What's wrong with the way you look? I didn't say anything's wrong with the way you look."

"You said I hadda get a cure. Do I look sick to you, *chiquita*?" Angelo couldn't help but smile to see the lilly-white girl from horse country turn red in his face, but he let the skin of his jaws drop so no one would notice.

"Oh you don't look that bad," and for the first time Chamber looked up from his sullen rock-star snit on the top of the stairs to see her say, "You're self-conscious is all."

"Well at least I'm better-looking than he is," Angelo pointed at Chamber's cracked face and wrapped-to-the-nose bandages.

She started to say, "No, you're not," but thought better of it. "I just thought of it so I said it. No biggie."

"No self-control."

"Really?" she said, throwing her head back and twisting her neck to the side. "Well I think I feel—"

Then everybody looked at Paige when they heard the sickly ripping sound.

"—like something really tough."

And the ripping got louder and turned gutteral. Paige lowered her head; the back of it was torn in a jagged path down underneath her loose T-shirt. There was no blood, but a glinting shiny something under the shreds of the girl's flesh. She shimmied under her clothes and twisted her right shoulder, holding her right hand down off the rail of the balcony. The casing of her arm all the way to the shoulder blade peeled off like snakeskin onto the floor.

"Euu, *gross*," Jubilee shrieked.

Everett cackled with laughter because he thought it looked so cool.

Angelo kept a poker face, staring down Paige as she metamorphosed because he thought it was the proper thing to do and besides, it gave him an excuse to watch because he thought it was really cool too.

Paige was a sweet, innocent, decent child as far as

Jono was concerned: quite the finest person he had met in America, perhaps in all his life. She was a vast moor covered in perfect white snow without a flaw in its shining blue-white surface. He looked up at her ripping away her outer layer of skin to replace it with sheer reflecting crystal and would have smiled if he had a mouth. He wanted to run through that perfect field of snow in heavy thigh boots and roll around in it until it was chunky and worn and comfortable.

Paige clutched the flap of her shirt in a diamond crystal hand and pulled up on it, tearing the seams as she tried yanking it over her head. She shed her shoes and red spandex school uniform as destructively. What remained of her epidermis fell on the floor.

"All right girl!" Everett howled and applauded.

She had said she felt like something really tough but she had never been this hard before. She felt like an athlete in the Zone as she twisted the hundred facets of her diamond mouth into the rictus of a smile. She turned her face so that her dense rock of a corn-fed turned-up nose brushed Angelo's floppy-skinned South-Central pug and scraped it across the bridge.

Softly, she said: "Boo!" swiping a diamond-edged set of fingernails across where Angelo's chest had been a moment before.

Skin took a step back and vaulted the railing of the balcony, dropping the twenty-odd feet to the floor below. He wrapped five thick tendrils of flesh extended from the fingers of his left hand around the horizontal bannister. As he went over it, he swung in an arc.

DIAMONDS IN THE ROUGH

But before Skin could light on the ground and retract his fingers, Paige flipped over the rail too, and hit the ground flat, landing on a diamond-hard butt. The hard-wood floor cracked and poked up through the Oriental rug—that Professor Xavier had once told Sean he had picked up at an estate auction at a "steal away price" of forty-five hundred dollars—which tore in the center.

Everett, grinning, crooked his elbow and waved his fist like an umpire calling a runner out. "Husk! Husk! Husk!" he chanted.

Jubilee skittered over the back of the couch and joined him: "Husk! Husk! Husk! Husk!"

Angelo kicked off a shoe and threw a foot upward at a slow-moving ceiling fan and wrapped his ankle flesh around the fan's post. He swung up toward the fan, avoiding a diamond-hard tackle from the girl as even Jono joined the refrain with Jubilee and Synch chanting, "Husk! Husk! Husk!"

As Skin retracted himself upward to hang by a leg below the fan, holding it still by blocking its rotation with his knee, Paige stood on the floor twenty-eight feet below him. She stood with her diamond hands on her diamond waist slowly blinking open-and-shut with her diamond eyelids making the slightest scraping noise along her tear ducts. She said, "You don't think so, do you?"

And with that she began scaling the rough-sawn pine wall like Spider-Man, creeping up by digging fingers and toes ever so slightly into the wood panels to triangulate herself upward foot-by-foot, inch-by-inch toward the dangling Angelo.

The other mutants continued to cheer: "Husk! Husk! Husk! Husk!"

Then the door of the headmaster's office flew open and out stomped Sean Cassidy followed by Monet St. Croix and Emma Frost. Everyone froze in place, waiting for the Banshee yell that could shatter diamond. Husk gulped.

"How many times do I have to tell you?" Sean said in a voice that was not a Banshee scream but nonetheless quite loud, "Not in the house!"

"Sorry man," said Angelo hanging from the ceiling fan.

"Uh . . . uh . . . sorry," said Paige hanging off the wall.

"We all apologize, sir," from Jono.

"Chamber," Sean addressed Jonothon, "why don't you fly on up to that fan and help your friend down?"

"Right away, sir."

Jubilee especially was disappointed to learn that the student body were not going off after super-villains in a time warp. Jono was non-committal, Paige still contrite especially when she saw the little pockmarks she had left in the wall and the rips in the rug no one had yet mentioned. All Sean had ordered Paige to do was put on a hospital gown in case she had a sudden compulsion to shed her diamond skin for her more accustomed flesh.

Angelo and Everett thought it would be a good time

to make themselves scarce, so without bringing it up in actual words they dropped a field trip request form in the slot outside Sean's office door. Before the meeting started, they had optimistically packed a few clothes for a weekend trip to Boston.

"Everybody here?" Sean asked his evidently recovered students who draped themselves over assorted chairs and couches in the sitting room of the main building. "Almost everybody here?"

Everybody was here except for Penance, who made even Jonothon feel less of a misanthrope. Penance had the gravitational pull of a tiny piece of a neutron star; you could feel it when she entered a room.

"Has anyone seen Penance today?" Sean asked.

Nobody had.

"Two items on the agenda today, lads and lassies," the headmaster continued. "A new student—"

Raised eyebrows and whispers among the half-dozen attending students of Xavier's School for Gifted Youngsters.

"—and an unidentified manifestation on our campus this morning."

"Manifestation?" Jubilee asked.

"What went on in the biosphere this morning," Jono told her.

"You said it was an alien invasion or something."

"No alien invasion. Just some kind of mirage or something. I was trying to tell you."

"You weren't trying very hard," Jubilee sniffed.

"What fun would that be?"

"I was hoping," Banshee reclaimed the floor, "that we were about done with fun for today."

The group was uncharacteristically well behaved this afternoon. The headmaster was not going to question his sudden good luck.

"Our new student is named Walter Nowland," Sean said, "and he's from a faraway and very flat land called Nebraska. I met and interviewed him and his family when I was in Chicago last month. Walter's a good lad and I think he'll fit in fine here. He'll arrive sometime today. His code name'll be Statis."

"Sounds like he's from like Beverly Hills or Scarsdale or something," said Angelo.

"Statis with an 'I'," Sean corrected, "not Status with a 'U'. Has to do with generating fields of static electricity."

"Gotcha," from Skin.

"Pretty original talent," Jubilee suggested with some sarcasm.

"Not nearly as useful," Paige cut in, hissing through diamond lips, "as, say, making fireworks out of your anxiety."

Jubilee squinted at Husk like a diamond-cutter.

"We've all got the talents we were born with," Emma reminded her students, "same as *homo sapiens*."

"Except we're superior," Monet pointed out, "technically speaking," she added primly.

"Let a Congressman hear you talking like that, young lassie," Sean warned, "and we'll be fighting off a whacko militia floating down the Mad River before you can say 'cultural warfare'."

Sean then related the story of the glowing egg in the biosphere, asking Emma and Monet to make any corrections if they felt any were necessary—which they did not. He said that long experience as a mutant had taught him and every X-Man the universal truth that big power attracts big trouble like tall trees attract lightning. He asked Jono if he had anything to add; Jono shrugged and said nothing.

"Is that it?" Jubilee asked impatiently. "I mean, I didn't really think we were going after time travelers—at least I don't think I really thought so—but I thought there was something worth going after. Not a cocka-mamie delusion."

Monet glared across the room at Jubilee, about to say something, but Emma beat her to it. "It was not a 'cock-amamie delusion,' as you so tastelessly put it, Jubilation. I saw it, and I sensed it."

"Do you all mean to tell me," Sean walked around the room with his arms on his hips and his head shaking, "that you're all so bloody bored and cabin fevered that you're disappointed we only have mirages in the garden?"

General murmured agreement.

Sean looked around at his charges for a few more beats, then threw his head back and laughed like no one had heard him laugh in months. "Welcome to winter in New England, lads and lassies. Get used to it. We convene again tonight to meet our new classmate. You've all got major papers due in the next two weeks, I expect you'll spend a good chunk of the rest of the day pounding them out. Except for you, Paige, you're due in the infirmary for analysis. Anyone sees Penance, let me know as usual. Dismissed.''

Somewhere in the air, a consciousness rose. It wafted among the pines and snowy surfaces of the estate, through the water under the ice, across the frozen surface of the forest where hibernating life readied itself to bloom and stretch. It floated through the odd compound of flora where it had first met the female, Emma Frost, and over the short expanse into the warren where the beings congregated.

The immature ones would be easy. And they were powerful indeed. The older male was strong willed but without sufficient imagination. He would be unavailable, but he would not be an impediment. Not as long as he remained indulgent of the weakness of the Frost female.

The consciousness took a sense of the surroundings: bucolic, pastoral. These beings found it beautiful, especially in relation to the whiteness outside. The phrase ''winter in New England'' had sent shudders of varying degrees through the sensibilities of the immature ones.

That would be useful as well.

Paige hated the infirmary, but at least she was used to it. She had her own routine. Whenever she metamorphosed, either spontaneously or on a lark as she had this time, she had to take all sorts of readings of her vitals to help Sean—and the powers-that-be back at the Xavier Institute in New York—to figure out how Paige could control her special talent.

She started with blood pressure, almost undetectable in her current state. She supposed that not only was blood flowing more slowly, but also that the meter couldn't get a reading through diamond-hard skin. And drawing her blood for testing was pretty much out of the question, she realized with relief. There were certainly a dozen other even grosser tests and samples she could take care of, though, and reluctantly she began to go about them.

Suddenly, she realized there was someone with her in the lab—a figure in shadow between a cabinet and the far wall. The shadow the cabinet cast seemed larger than before.

"Hello?" Paige called.

And Penance clattered out from the corner, dragging most of the shadow with her.

Penance had no other name that anyone was sure of, except Yvette, and that might have been something Emplate made up. From what they could determine, she was perhaps fourteen years old. She had little history other than as a slave to Emplate, the tyrant who sucked on mutants' life-force in order to live and found in Penance someone who could survive to be fed on another day.

Penance seemed bigger than she was; in fact she was smaller than Jubilee. But her mass was enormous. She was as dense as the compressed core of the Earth and her physiology reflected that: limbs and digits that were collapsed into long pointed tendrils; a face that was a gaunt death mask; ribbons of hair like the barbed coils that top electrified fences. Her very touch on normal flesh could be disastrous, like the hoof of a mule trying to touch a bead of dew on a rose petal. She was always in shadow. Light seemed not to reflect off her smooth features.

Emma stuck her head in the infirmary door. "Paige, did you call for—oh." She stopped at the sight of the girl approaching Husk.

When Sean had first freed Penance from Emplate's bondage and enrolled her at the school, she responded with hostility. She resisted any attempt he made to talk with her, realizing somehow that his voice was also his weapon. At one point, she nearly vivisected Sean with her fingertips. Since then, though she had been assigned a room, no one knew if she had ever stayed in it. In fact, no one knew where and how she spent most of her time. Every once in awhile one of the girls—Jubilee had been especially good that way—would just talk to her, without any idea whether she understood a word. Sometimes this seemed to comfort her a bit. Sometimes not.

Penance shuffled slowly toward the many-faceted Paige, leaving a trail of pockmarks on the tile infirmary floor as she moved.

"Sean," Emma called down the hall as gently and quietly as she could and still have the sound travel, "it's Penance. In the infirmary."

"For heaven's sake," and the headmaster barrelled

down the hall into the entrance of the room.

"Wait," said Emma and put a hand on his beefy arm. And he did.

Half a dozen adolescent heads popped in behind Sean and Emma, wondering what was going on. As they all watched, Penance—her deadly arms extended—shambled toward Paige, in diamond skin and a hospital gown.

"What?" Sean was apprehensive but Emma tightened her hand on his forearm.

And Penance wrapped her arms around the diamond-hard skin of Paige—who had never managed to turn to something this resilient before—and rested her head on the diamond shoulder. And Paige hugged Penance back.

With each squeeze, Paige's diamond flesh began to crack and chip, but she did not break the embrace.

"What?" Sean said again, and noticed a smile on the White Queen's face—but not her usual smile, the one that looked like a feral animal about to devour its prey. This was a genuine smile, and the beginnings of a tear started to pool in her ice-blue eyes—both were rare phenomena with Emma Frost.

"Do you have any idea," Emma said, "how long it must be since that child has been hugged?"

And Penance and Paige held each other that way for many minutes, until a fissure appeared in Paige's diamond surface to signal the return of the girl's perfect soft skin. They all left to give Paige some privacy. Penance seemed reluctant to go.

After the transformation, Paige went to her room to

dress. She ran back to the infirmary, but Penance was gone.

Sighing, she went out into the snow to jog along the riverbank, alone.

CHAPTER THREE

PUNCTUATED EQUILIBRIUM

In Stockbridge, Harley Nowland had stopped for gas. "Think we're close, Wally?" he asked his son who huddled under a blanket in the front seat.

"Dunno."

"Maybe get directions, y'think?"

"'Kay."

"Think I should tell them where we're really going?"

"Dunno."

Harley Nowland sat in the car at the self-serve pump for a moment, while his son Walter shivered in the blankets next to him. He should have put the boy on a plane for heaven's sake like Dora said. A long road trip like this can only make things worse.

"Maybe I should just get a road map, y'think, Wally?"

"'Kay."

"Sir, can I help you with something?" The smiley young face hovered outside the window less than a foot from Harley's nose. "This is the self-serve pump."

"Right," Harley said, getting out of the old 1979 Delta 88. The boy wore a green jump suit, the name "Tim" embroidered in yellow thread over his pocket.

"Know how to use the pump, sir?" Tim asked.

"I guess I do, son," Harley grinned. "You don't drive from Nebraska to Massachusetts in four days without knowing how to use a gas pump."

"All the way from Nebraska in this old beauty?"

"Beauty is right. She ain't what she used to be. No

trouble these last four days, though. Highway driving blows those tubes right out, yessir.''

Tim smiled and turned to go back into the station but Harley stopped him.

"Hey fella, there is something you could do for me if you would.''

"Yes sir.''

"You guys sell maps?''

"Yes sir. Massachusetts and Connecticut, including metropolitan Boston, Hartford, and New Haven, New York State with metropolitan New York, and a detail of the upper Hudson River Valley, New Hampshire, and Vermont, and I think we've got a couple of Maines left with the Maritime Provinces.''

"Local,'' Harley finally stopped him. "Local's fine. We're real local now, I think.''

"Straight up, sir.''

Tim hotfooted it into the station as Harley filled the tank with regular unleaded. They didn't sell leaded gas much outside the Midwest any more. Harley'd blown his catalytic converter off with an acetylene torch years ago and put a wider funnel under his gas cap so he could get the cheaper fuel in. Didn't do the air supply any good but it sure saved Harley a few bucks. This trip hadn't, though. What with food on the road—Walter was partial to fast food—motels every night because the kid got the chills, and all the cough medicine he had to buy along the way, these four days had cost easily as much as a plane ticket. And now he would have to drive back to Nebraska alone.

Harley paid Tim for the gas and the map and Tim sprayed and washed the Olds' windshields as Harley puzzled over the arrangement of the roads before him. The hamlet of Snow Valley was a tiny open black circle to the north of Route 9. There was a little access road called Route 9A that jagged off the main thoroughfare to bisect the little circle and merge right back in, but there were no roads going in or out of Snow Valley anywhere else. That Cassidy fellow that Dora thought was such a trustworthy guy had clearly said "North of Snow Valley," but there was nothing north of Snow Valley. The Mass Pike ran east and west a good seven or eight miles to the north, on the other side of what looked to be a wooded area with a few creeks and three or four small mountains. North of that was Route 20 heading west into New York state and east to Boston.

Well, Harley supposed he would just go to Snow Valley and ask and hope for the best.

Outside, Tim finished spit-shining the windows and saluted smartly, stepping back to signal Harley on his way. Next to Harley, his son Walter shivered and coughed. It depressed him, and being depressed reminded Harley to lose the puzzled look and contrive a grin for the boy's benefit. Harley went to start up the car and all the key in the ignition did was click.

Harley sighed despite himself. "We're out of charge. Knew I shouldn't've let you watch the TV plugged into the lighter. Ain'tcha had enough of Kathie Lee Gifford for one lifetime?"

Immediately Harley realized he'd blown the whole

show of normalcy he was trying to create for the boy's benefit. Certainly at sixteen, Walter Nowland had not had enough of anything for one lifetime.

After an uncomfortable beat Walter said, "Dunno."

So here Harley was, stranded in a twenty-year-old car in a New England winter with a sick teenager. Good thing they were at a gas station. Harley figured that even if this "Tim" person couldn't translate that grin into mechanical know-how he could at least let Harley use the tools in his garage and rig something up. But instead, Walter reached a tattooed left hand out from under his blanket toward the empty lighter socket on the dashboard.

"Leave the key in, Dad," Walter said, and a tiny bolt of electricity from Walter's long bony forefinger bathed the interior of the empty lighter cylinder in blinding white light and turned its surface black. The car shuddered. Harley, leaning his bare arm on the metal of the car door, felt the hair on his head and arms stiffen. Then the old car started up and purred like a kitten.

"Excuse me, sir?" Tim tapped on the window on Walter's side as Harley was about to drive away.

Harley leaned over his son and rolled down the window a crack.

"Did you find what you were looking for on the map, sir?"

"Well close enough I suppose."

"Don't go anywhere," and Tim ran back into the station to come right out with a rolled up tube of paper in his hand. "A little sideline of mine," he said as he handed the tube of paper through Harley's window.

Harley slid off the paper collar holding it together and unrolled a decorated tourist map of the Berkshire Hills Recreation Area. There was the Butternut Basin Ski Area, Tanglewood, the site of Alice's Restaurant memorialized in the Arlo Guthrie song, and, straddling the banks of a narrow stream that came down from one of the Berkshires just north of Snow Valley, a little smudge of land the map called "Xavier's School," with a nameless dead end road leading into it from Route 9A.

"More like it," Harley told Tim. "What do I owe you, pal?"

"On the house," Tim said. "Maybe when the kid's feeling better he can come help out in the garage."

Even Walter managed a smile before they drove off.

Paige thought she could navigate the crooked banks of the Mad River blindfolded at a dead run. Sometimes, running around a blind corner through the woods, she closed her eyes as she pounded the dirt and rocks for as long as she could stand it, just to prove it to herself. She hadn't tripped up yet. She had been here since the beginning of last summer and she thought she had seen all the moods of this quick, shallow river.

When she had first met this stream flowing down from the mountain it seemed rather lazy. It flowed in an even, steady rhythm under, over, around, and through the debris and undergrowth of the woods, down the occasional little cascade. It slowed over the months into a trickle. Then with the autumn rains, it grew again and even muddied its banks with overflow and seepage for days after a storm ended.

In November and December the forest gradually slowed and the river flow virtually stopped. It iced over, and a shifting blanket of snow covered the ice. And for months, only the face of the snow and the occasional falling tree trunk surrendered to the pressure of change.

Today, there was only a thin membrane of ice along the edges of the river; in the center, water flowed easily. Still, the forest was heavy with snow and great branches sagged under its weight.

The sound of the river, along with her familiarity with the twists and dips of this place, guided Paige as she jogged along the river with a three-pound weight in each fist. She kept her eyes shut longer than she ever had before. She was home, navigating the snowy forest as easily as a blind man finds his way among the furniture in his living room. Paige opened her eyes only when she heard a sound that didn't belong here.

She heard purring.

A large boulder sat in the middle of the river, on which stood the hazy figure of a tall purple-haired woman in a red jump suit. She was hazy, indistinct. Her edges faded into the backdrop of the woods, but Paige could swear the girl had a tail snaking around behind her.

"You're Catseye," Paige said to the figure. One of the now-deceased Hellions, Paige remembered her both from the school's files as well as the descriptions from her older brother Sam. Sam, aka Cannonball, was a member of the New Mutants, the previous group of trainee mutants at the Xavier Institute, at the same time that the Hellions were active.

The woman crouched on her haunches and began to transform. In a moment, radiating from her middle, her figure became that of an enormous cat; like a purple lynx with a bobbed tail and densely muscular haunches with which the creature sprung directly at Paige, claws extended, even as she transformed.

She was much more distinct as a cat. Seeing her transform was like adjusting the contrast on a television screen. The air tingled around Paige—or was it just the after-effects of her last transformation? She didn't know, and she probably shouldn't be thinking about it just now. What was all this jogging and training and conditioning for? What was the purpose of all these lectures from Banshee about being ready for any eventuality? It was all so that when a monster appeared out of the wilderness—as was monsters' wont—Paige could deal with it.

Paige sprung out of the way with the cat-thing in mid-spring.

The creature flew claws-first right where Paige had stood. She could smell a wet fur smell as she flew by her, hissing, directly at the tree trunk. Then the cat vanished into the air as though going into an invisible door inches in front of the tree.

The dining hall, after the others had all finished dinner and cleared the big table:

"You're still thinking about the Hellions," Sean said, noticing Emma's dark mood.

"Now you're telepathic?" Emma chided.

"Doesn't take a telepath."

"They were too young."

"We're all too young," Sean said. "George Burns was too young. Irving Berlin was too young. Grandma Moses was too young. Wolverine's too young."

"Philosophy doesn't become you, Sean," Emma said icily, "and your analogy doesn't hold up. I wasn't responsible for George Burns's death."

"Weren't you, by your reasoning?" Sean posed.

"George Burns died of old age a few weeks after his hundredth birthday."

"You hustled to try to save the Hellions," Sean said, "but you didn't run off to Beverly Hills to feed George Burns hot chicken soup and take him for his daily walks when you heard he'd turned a hundred."

"I wasn't responsible for the life of George Burns!" Emma snapped. "I *was* responsible for the Hellions—for their lives, and for their deaths."

Sean paused, realizing that his flippancy was ill-timed. He started to erect the logical roadblocks he would need to construct in the path of his colleague's chronic self-flagellation. He did not get the chance, however, because Emma suddenly cocked her head, listening inside it, and said, "Our new student."

She pushed aside her uneaten roughage. Sean heard a car pulling into the driveway, kicking up gravel and corn snow as it came.

GENERATION X

* * *

Walter Nowland seemed reserved, contained—quite unlike the bubbling, outgoing young man Sean had interviewed in Chicago. Emma could offer no suggestions; evidently something about the powerful static charges he emitted blocked her. However, she did notice, as the young boy took off his heavy jacket, the tattoos that lined his arms. She raised her eyebrows. Sean noticed Emma's expression and smiled.

Sean had discussed Walter's tattoos with him when they had met several weeks ago. "My father once said that there are two kinds of folk in the world," Sean had told Walter when they met back then. "There are people with tattoos and people who are afraid of being hit by people with tattoos."

"Your father must've been a Dick Van Dyke fan," the kid told him.

"My dad never heard of Dick Van Dyke as far as I know. We never had television in Ireland until I was about your age."

"Bet the first thing you got was American reruns."

"Yeah, that's right."

"I remember one episode of that show," the tattooed boy said. "Laura once got her big toe stuck in the bathtub faucet and Rob had to get a guy with a hacksaw to—"

"Yes!" Sean suddenly reunited with an episode of his childhood. "All you saw through the whole show was her head peeking out behind the shower curtain. Dad loved that show!"

PUNCTUATED EQUILIBRIUM

From then on Walter and Sean got on famously. Walter then confided that he'd gotten his first tattoo when he was nine and his mother fainted. After that, dealing with his mutant power to generate electrical fields and burn rubber with his bare hands was not such a big deal.

Now Sean studied Walter carefully to see what had changed. He looked like the same boy Sean had sparred and laughed with in Chicago those weeks ago. He just didn't carry himself the same way. He was fairly tall, with long hair that hung around his shoulder tops.

Harley, Walter's father, was long, narrow, and weathered, like a Nebraska highway. His hair was as blond as his son's, but there was only a fringe of it left along the borders of his scalp.

"Your room's the second door on the left up this hall. It's all yours," Sean said to Walter, "no roommates."

"Thank you very much," Harley said as Walter absently ran his hands along the wall as he floated toward the room.

"Ms. Frost and I can help you get settled if you—"

"Ain't got much stuff," Harley said. "Just a satchel of dirty clothes. We'll take care of it ourselves if you don't mind."

"Y'know, Mr. Nowland," Sean grinned, "I was just going to order a load of clothes for the kids. Seems somebody left a bucketful of diamond chips all over the infirmary floor. Found money for the school. Don't worry about a thing."

"Diamond chips?" asked Harley. "You serious, Cassidy?"

"Actually, yes. Transmutation accident."

Walter disappeared into his room with Harley behind him. "Whatever," Harley said as he shut the door.

"Different lad, he seems," Sean confided to Emma outside the house on the path to the biosphere. Despite the snow, the day was too warm to see their breaths.

"You mean unusual?" she asked.

"No more than any adolescent mutant. He just seems more self-involved and quiet now."

"I can't get through to him either for some reason." Then Emma stopped. "Wait a minute."

"What?"

"I'm getting something. There's something wrong."

"With Walter?"

"I think—"

And before she could finish, a branch of the snow-encrusted Scotch pine under which they stood tumbled out of the sky. Crusted crystals of settled snow whipped down from it around Sean's cheeks for just an instant less than the time it would have taken for Banshee's reflexes to have catapulted him out of the way of the dense, ice-logged branch that clapped him on the skull and threw him off his feet.

"No, I guess it was something else," Emma said drily as she helped Sean back to his feet.

Then they heard a deep belly laugh from somewhere above.

High in the tree, in a black and purple haze, was the figure of a man as dense and thick as the branch he'd apparently tumbled down on Banshee's head.

"Beef?" Emma whispered and the figure faded away.

"Another one of your late charges?" Banshee asked, blinking.

"Yes. Did you see him?"

"I'm not sure."

Banshee felt a rhythmic clapping underneath his feet. Instinctively, he rattled his head and stretched his throat, ready to loose a holler that could turn the iron core of the Earth.

Along the footpath by the side of the frozen river, Paige ran toward home with her weights in her fists. Banshee and the White Queen stepped from behind their tree, Sean still picking pine needles out from under the collar of his shirt.

"Hey you guys," Paige called, excited, "guess what I saw?"

"A dead Hellion?" asked Sean. Emma shot him a look to rebuke his insensitivity, which he declined to notice.

"Yeah, Catseye. She nearly clawed me to ribbons. Isn't it awful?" Her tone clearly said, *Isn't it cool?*

Harley Nowland took off, telling only his son that he was leaving. Walter showed for the evening meeting just long enough to be introduced, and then Sean let it out early. He glossed over the encounters that he, Emma, and Paige had with what seemed to be the ghosts of the lost Hellions. He also agreed to Everett and Angelo's request for a Boston excursion.

The kids all tore off to their rooms and Sean exca-
vated his office for the keyboard to his computer. He
whipped out his web browser, tapped out the URL for
L.L. Bean, and hit ENTER.

With the expansion of the Internet, Banshee had discovered a new passion. As long as he could do it sitting
in his big comfortable office chair in front of a web
browser, he loved to shop. No trying stuff on. No waiting around for some salesperson to tell him what he or
she thought. No bopping around from store to store
looking over a million pairs of shoes just to make sure
the first pair you saw was really what you wanted.

Sean punched in the secret code that activated the
school's credit card account and threw papers from his
second desk drawer onto the floor until he found a list
of all of his students' clothing sizes. He ordered two
dozen chamois shirts and ten pairs of leather ankle boots.
He ordered all sorts of fleece stuff including an armload
of new sweat suits and a couple of pairs of hiking boots
for Jubilee and Husk. He got in-line skates, pads, and
half-a-dozen helmets for Synch and new lightweight
mountain bikes for M and the White Queen. He got a
few heavy thermal outfits for Skin who could use the
extra support and liked everything about New England
but the climate. For Penance he thought a minute and
ordered a pair of Rossignol cross-country skis, a few
extra pairs of poles, and a geodesic one-person tent; if
he kept getting her stuff, there was always hope the girl
would develop an interest in something. For Chamber
he pulled down another backcountry one-person tent,

some winter hiking gear, and the fattest Swiss army knife they made, the one with the little needle woven into the corkscrew. And finally, he hauled in a truckload of fly-fishing gear for Statis, the new kid: rods, reels, boxes full of gear, and one of those floppy hats in which to stick all of his hooks and lures.

Federal Express would deliver his merchandise bright and early Monday morning. Banshee loved to shop.

"Perhaps now would be a good time to speak to Walter." Emma appeared behind him. It was not a question.

"Is that a telepathic thing?"

"No, it's a woman thing."

Sean didn't much like it when his headmistress finished conversations he was having with his unconscious, but he agreed. He spent the next three or four hours in Walter's room listening and talking about the boy's secret.

A little after midnight the rain started.

A few minutes before dawn, a black-clad figure rode a pillar of white heat through the storming skies. Jono wore a harness and an aluminum cone from his chest to his ankles. He could direct the psionic energy out the bottom of his chamber in a jetstream. With this rig he could actually fly, albeit slowly and for short distances. If he tried to go much farther or any faster than a person could walk, he would burn his own feet. He found a perch high in a good solid oak with a long view of the Mad River raging downstream. Here, Chamber sat and watched an annual event.

One day a year—every single year—the river broke and the face of the land changed. Under the first good rain of March, the ice at the tops of two mountains that formed the source of the Mad River cracks, pretty much simultaneously. That cracked ice weighs against the ice downriver. Eventually, a tiny floe of melting ice drops against a slightly bigger loosening floe at the intersection of two little trickles. The weight of it all builds up speed until a bundle of cracked ice tumbles through the point where the stream down one mountain meets the stream down the other. Then river run starts in earnest. The ice starts picking up gravel and stones and moves a little faster. A rock hits an unmelted chunk of ice that breaks in a clean chunk and tumbles up and onto a cracking spot and picks up speed. The pressure of breaking up melts the ice and pushes a little harder. By the time the cracking ice under the first spring rain reaches the point where the Mad River widens enough to look like a river, water and ice and tumbling debris are screaming along at breakneck speed and the very land is subject to the vicious moods of the bending river.

Once upon a time, when Jonothon was a little boy he read a thrilling story about a man who was so powerful he could "change the course of mighty rivers." It happened here every year.

Boulders traveled downriver bouncing against the banks, widening them. A tree clapped at the base of its trunk by a wad of frozen dirt leapt up into the air and left an enormous hole where its root had been for a hundred and sixty years. The river clambered hard into the hole and pressed against it with spume after spume of torrential waters until its course changed. Before the day and the storm were done, the course of this river would move half a mile to the east.

Sometime around a hundred thousand years ago, *homo sapiens* supplanted Cro Magnon and Neanderthal and every other competing hominid race on the planet and it seems to have happened in just a few generations. Human genes had not changed one whit in that time. True, people were nearly a foot taller now than they were five hundred years ago, but twenty-thousand years ago humans averaged five-feet-eleven and then lost more than a foot when they stopped being hunter-gatherers and started farming the land and eating too many carbohydrates. It has taken a thousand generations to get that foot back, and human DNA still has not changed its essential nature.

Until the twentieth century.

Now *homo sapiens* were spontaneously giving birth to *homo superior* and the races had to learn to live together or it could all happen again.

There were groups of dunderheads popping up in all the major cities who called themselves "Friends of Humanity." They were an anti-mutant hate organization. They had meetings and rallies and wrote letters to newspapers and magazines and trained in the woods with automatic ordnance and occasionally got someone elected to something. Their consciousnesses knew nothing but resentment and fear—but the perception in the depths of their souls that gave birth to that resentment and fear told them that they were doomed. They were people out of their depth in a shallow gene pool.

Inevitably, *homo superior* would win out, one way or another. But the generation of whom Jonothon Starsmore and his schoolmates were a member were the pioneers. They were the ones who had to deal with the Friends of Humanity and the hostile governments and the apocalyptic pseudoscientists. Jonothon's generation were the ones who had to try to make peace because, as the world stood today, it belonged to humanity. Jono hated being a pioneer. And unlike *homo sapiens* of a hundred thousand years ago, Jono and his generation of mutants could not, in this world, go off in a quiet secret cave and give birth to an army in the dark.

No matter how inviting that image was.

A big old tree came rolling downriver roots and all, caught in a jam between two boulders and water started rolling up and over it like a spout. The Mad River had crested its banks hours ago and the ground below the oak where Chamber perched and all the ground for a quarter-mile to either side of him was awash in angry Mad River and melting snowpack. It was all Jono could do to take it all in.

"I love that river," Paige had told him once. "I've seen the Mad River in all its moods." The girl was a love but she wouldn't recognize a cliché if it bit her on the butt. He should go back to the main building and get her and show her this mood.

It was easy for Jono to think about Paige. Her florid

cheeks. Her wild flaxen hair. The roll of her shoulders.

Then that tree that was wedged in those boulders was suddenly free and flying violently through the storm—through the air toward Jono in his tree—roots-first. And perched atop the flying roots, riding it and hollering like Slim Pickens on the shaft of the H-bomb in the last scene of *Dr. Strangelove*, was a woman in purple and black and wavy blonde hair that the rain didn't faze. And she was tossing little black and white disks at him one after the other that faded into nothingness before they reached him. But the tree. . . .

It was too close. It was in his face. He could blow it from the sky and himself to Kingdom Come, but instead he could—

—snatch it!

He rode the root of the enormous missile up into the sky. He had to shed his flying mechanism by hugging the flying tree with one arm and loosing the harness from the other, then repeating the process with the other arm. By the time he clambered up over the soaking filthy roots to the upper side of it the thing had crashed through the roof of the woods and reached the top of its arc. And the blonde woman was gone.

He got his balance, kicked off upward and fired up his Chamber.

Up, up through the storm he rose out of control like a balloon losing its air as the tree came flopping down through the sopping forest, tossing aside branches and twigs as it fell, dismembering a couple of cords of hardwood before it clattered across the raging river and settled in a ditch of its own making. Jono came down like a rock but softened his fall by shooting out spits of psionic force at the ground, bouncing in ever-shorter bumps until he touched down on a rock outcropping just upriver of the tumbled old tree.

By tomorrow afternoon when the waters recede, Jonothon thought, *that sucker'll make a fine sturdy bridge.* The tree had reached an equilibrium with its environment. Soon the rest of the forest would follow, at least for another year. Then he noticed the time. He could not forget morning roll call—that always made Sean aggravated for the rest of the day.

CHAPTER FOUR

THE WAGES OF DESPAIR

Everett and Angelo came down to breakfast with their bags packed. They traveled light: Everett had a satchel full of clothes and a pair of Nikes laced together through the handles, Angelo carried only a hip-pack stuffed with his wallet and seven changes of underwear.

"I'm starting to feel seriously stifled around here," Angelo whispered to Everett as they came down the stairs to the main room.

"You too?" said Everett. "Cabin fever, huh?"

"Could be. Everywhere but here, spring's breaking out. You hear it hit seventy in Boston yesterday?"

"I'm there, brother mine."

They spoke softly. Only Emma could hear them and she was not listening to much of anything.

The Hellions were calling her to muster. Nothing else mattered.

Emma couldn't focus. That was one of her best things, focus. Other than her hair and her collection of shoes. She had great shoes. Lots of them. But other than that one of her best things was . . .

What was she thinking about?

One of her best things.

What were her best things?

Her money? Lots of money. Where did she keep that now?

And her hair and her shoes.

Emma looked down at her shoes. Tan and navy waterproof Gore-Tex dayhikers. Eighty-five dollars. What the well-dressed telepath will wear. Especially in mud season in rural New England.

Emma stood up to look at her hair in the big mirror over the fireplace in the meeting room. Not bad. She ought to get out more often. She probably wouldn't.

"Well we're almost all here," Sean said. Walter hadn't arrived, and Sean wanted to wait until he showed.

Each morning, the students convened in the living room. First came the daily gab session. Sean always steered the conversation around to what the students had learned the previous day. He found mornings the best time to examine each student's activities so they could receive constructive criticism on their actions. What with M's aloofness, Skin's sarcasm, Chamber's general depression, and Jubilee's attitude, it never seemed to work out that way. But he could always hope.

After the conversation talked itself out, the students got into their red uniforms and went to the biosphere for their workout. Sometimes he'd work with the whole group, sometimes with individuals. Always trying to hone their strengths, always trying to eliminate their weaknesses. Those not active would, presumably, concentrate on their homework. Then after the biosphere session came four hours of classes in history, the arts, and science.

Sean Cassidy was proud of his students. He knew they worked harder, both physically and mentally, than other students.

GENERATION X

Today, however, there were more immediate problems to discuss. His train of thought was interrupted by a shuffling noise from the hallway. Chamber vaulted over the back of the couch where he sat to throw open the hallway door. There stood Walter, leaning against a wall catching his breath. Jono assisted him into the room.

"Always the hero, huh?" Walter smiled, standing erect again.

"Force of habit," said Chamber.

Sean assessed the room. Everyone seemed kind of draped over the furniture, rather than sitting in it. Sean never felt that it was his job to teach these kids manners. That was their parents' job, or the job of their earlier teachers. Still, a little decorum might be in order.

Oh, what did it matter?

"Well now we're really almost all here," Sean went on, "and most likely Penance is somewhere within earshot. I'd like to discuss the ghost-like manifestations most of us have been exposed to lately."

"Is that really why we're here?" Monet wanted to know. It was unlike her of all people, Sean thought, to interrupt and belittle an idea even before anyone had fully expressed it. "You want us to talk about ghosts?"

"Well, actually, yes Monet. I do."

"'Smatter, *chiquita*," Angelo said, "got a hot date?"

"Keep your blowhard mouth to yourself, wart-face!" Jubilee snapped at Angelo, who in response grabbed his lips, pulled them far from the rest of his face, waving them up and down at Jubilation like a fleshy jump rope.

"Euu, gross!" she said and blew a flare in front of his face that might have blinded him for a few moments if his flapping lips had not covered his eyes.

Sean shouted from deep in his sonic gut and the walls rattled and the furniture clattered across the floor with the kids in it. After that, it was quiet again. "Thank you," he said in a normal voice.

Monet said, "I was just suggesting that our time might be better spent if—"

"Your time will be better spent," Sean said sternly, "if you follow your headmaster's agenda before you present unwarranted conclusions of your own."

Except for Walter, everyone had seen a dead Hellion. Just today, Paige had come across Jetstream sitting in the big walk-in refrigerator. Paige squealed and ran from the room, leaving the refrigerator door hanging open. She immediately came back in and saw that there was in fact no human projectile sitting anywhere near here.

Jubilee found Tarot sitting by the artesian well. The Hellion who made images on tarot cards come alive tossed one of a naked woman pouring water into a well—the "Star" card from the Major Arcana—at her when she went to wash her muddied feet in the outdoor spigot after bouncing on the trampoline for forty-five minutes. For a moment the card floating through the air became three-dimensional, like a hologram. Then both Tarot and her naked water woman disappeared. Jubilee almost believed they had never been there and turned on the spigot. When she put one bare foot under the flow of water it was scalding hot and she tumbled onto the ground holding her toes.

Everett came across Bevatron at the old granite quarry out between the woods and the Mass Pike. He had gone there earlier, he said, to sit and wait for the morning to blow over.

"What do you mean by that?" Chamber snapped.

"What do you mean, what do I mean?" Everett asked back.

"What needs to be blowing over, is what I mean."

"Your cruddy mood."

"All right, all right," Sean interrupted. "Did the manifestation do any lasting damage?"

"No," Everett said. "Blew a couple of big granite rocks apart. One of them ricocheted and hit me in the throat, but I healed it with willpower."

"You can heal yourself with willpower now?" Monet asked, condescendingly.

"Yeah, I can do a lot of things nobody knows about yet," Everett snapped back. "Want to see me fix your tongue after some well-meaning suitor rips it out of its socket just to get some relief?"

"Oh, you're so vile." M turned her head away.

"Cut it out, you guys." That came from Walter whom, after all, nobody here really knew very well.

They all looked at him, as though expecting he had more to say.

He obliged them with a terse, "What?"

* * *

THE WAGES OF DESPAIR

They were fighting, Emma knew. Arguing, really, over whatever they felt like arguing about. *It doesn't matter*, she supposed. *We'd all be landfill pretty soon anyway.* Maybe she would go up to her room and read some Sartre until the young Hellions she had fed to the wolves came and carried her away with them where she belonged.

What's with Emma? Sean wondered. Not a word from the woman through all this. He would ponder this circumstance awhile longer until he realized he was not intervening either.

Some adult supervision, he mused, and failed to intervene some more.

The discussion had deteriorated from half a dozen reports of supposed Hellion-sightings to a series of nasty contradictions over what was behind them:

"—ghosts are haunting the old place—"

"—there's no such thing as ghosts—"

"—this isn't worth our attention—"

"—we've got better things to do—"

"—if they're ghosts, then they can't do anything to us anyway—"

And so forth.

Finally Walter said, "You're wrong, all of you."

"What are we wrong about, electro-boy?" Angelo wanted to know.

Walter said, "All of the above. There are no ghosts here, but there's something. Something certainly worth your time. I've felt it since I got here. Been resisting it, but I don't have the energy for it much longer. We've got to get to the bottom of it before it gets to the bottom of us.''

''What are you talking about?'' Everett wanted to know. ''What do you know about ghosts?''

''I know a lot about ghosts.''

''Well I know a lot about dark sinister forces, Statis. I've seen them since I was a kid,'' the thirteen-year-old Jubilee insisted. ''When I was with the X-Men—''

''No,'' Walter put up his hand. Everyone was shocked at how thin and bony his wrist was. No one had noticed that before. ''No,'' he said, ''you don't.''

''So what if it is ghosts?'' from Chamber. ''So they throw tree limbs and tarot cards at us. So what?''

''There's a force here,'' Walter said. ''I know because it's something I feel and I've never felt before.''

''Sounds like ghosts to me,'' Chamber said. ''Out on the moors back home there are all sorts of stories about—''

''I'm not talking about stories,'' Walter interrupted.

''Sorry.'' Jono was the only one in the room who had thought to apologize about anything this day.

''I know what ghosts feel like and this isn't it.''

''Really?'' from four kids simultaneously.

''I knew a ghost,'' Walter said. ''His name was Hiram. Now he's disappointed in me.''

''Hiram, the friendly ghost, the friendliest ghost you know,'' Jubilee suddenly started to sing until she realized nobody thought it was funny. Then she went back to sulking and disagreeing in general some more.

"Disappointed?" Paige asked. "How? Why?"

"I've got the Legacy Virus," Walter said, as though he had meant to say it casually. "Don't have a clue how I came down with it, but there it is. Screws up all Hiram's hard work, too."

Everyone was silent for a moment. Jubilation said, "Bummer." Monet flashed her a dirty look, mistakenly thinking the younger girl was making light of it. Jube couldn't help the way she talked; she had grown up in Encino, after all. But she'd already lost one friend, Il-lyana Rasputin, to the virus.

"Are you certain?" Jono wanted to know.

"I confirmed it last night with Hank McCoy." Sean spoke for the first time since the conversation had deteriorated. "He hasn't got much time, but he's chosen to spend it with us."

No one had anything they could think of to say after that.

Sean decided that tempers were too high for the usual daily sessions, so he dismissed the students for the weekend. Ten minutes later, Everett and Angelo found the oldest, rattliest of the half-dozen Jeep Wranglers that Sean kept in the converted carriage house by the gate. Their moods seemed to lift even as they tossed their light luggage into the back and piled themselves into the front seat. Everett turned the key in the ignition.

"What was that about, bro'?" Angelo asked.

"I don't know," Everett said as he punched the key

code into the gate control. "Ghosts got the school or something. And that mutant virus again, hey?"

The gate swung open and the old heap rattled out with the two boys aboard.

"Bummer," one of them said, and by the time they hit Route 9A neither could remember which of them had said it.

Just leaving was like lifting an enormous weight off both their souls. By the time they got to Sturbridge they thought of calling home to tell the rest of the gang to take a few days away. But even that idea melted off like the last corn snow of spring.

CHAPTER FIVE
STATIS

Walter had always lived in a haunted house—or, rather, on a haunted ranch. In the old farmhouse, pencils would walk across the table. Drapes used to shimmer as if with a breeze when the windows were closed. Dessert disappeared if you left it on the table when you went to turn on the television. Once in a while, the family would come home and find the dishes in the cabinets sitting in pieces. Dora would shuffle Walter and his brothers and sister out into the dooryard while Harley gave the house a good talking-to.

"All right, Hiram," Harley would say to the empty building, "I know you're around here somewhere."

Harley would look around, hoping to see the ranch hand who had been trampled in a cattle stampede when Harley's grandfather owned the spread. He had not seen the ghost in two years and was jealous when one of the kids said they caught sight of the old geezer.

"This is our place now," Harley went on, "not yours. And those dishes were the third set you've done in since the summer. I want you to lay off the family heirlooms—or what's left of them anyway. I want you to live and let live or so help me I'll level this place and start again. I'll get an exorcist and then where'll you be, hey? I'm gonna borrow Aunt Teddi's videocassette player and rent that movie if you break any more stuff. That'll put the fear of man in you."

By the time Harley finished his lecture, he was emotionally exhausted and screaming at the top of his lungs about green split-pea soup and throwing people out windows. Dora carried the baby and shuffled uncomfortably in front of her kids in the drive as Harley swaggered out of the house. "Won't see him again soon," he said as he escorted his family into the house. "Not for a long time, no sir."

Walter looked up at his dad, then behind him, and grinned.

"Whatcha looking at, Wally?" Harley said. Then he realized what was going on. "That china hound standing there behind me, boy?"

Walter nodded, smiling.

"Hell!" Harley slashed and slid, flailing at the air behind him as the laughing ghost of Hiram the hired hand faded from Walter's view.

There were no dishes left, so the family piled into the big Oldsmobile and went into town for a pizza. Walter was seven at the time.

Within a year Harley actually did make good on one of the threats he routinely tossed over the ghost of Hiram. He built a new ranch house a quarter-mile up the hill from the chicken-coop-cum-farmhouse and invited the neighborhood over to yank down the old post-and-beam building the day after he moved Dora and the kids into the new one. The Nowlands had a huge barbecue to celebrate the new house and, secretly among themselves, the demise of the ghost of the old hired hand.

For his part, Hiram had no trouble finding his way to the new house. He happily rattled furniture and dropped dishware and howled through the uncaulked corners of the building before the paint dried. Walter had invited him.

Walter Nowland's boyhood was a circus of horses and calf roping and shooting rattlers on the prairie and a home on the range. It was every kid's impossible dream. The cattle business was thin and nasty in those years, and Mom and Dad were broke silly most of the time, but that never concerned Walter or his siblings. There was plenty of food, plenty of friends, plenty of stuff to read, and, in his spare time, Walter kicked around in the garage among Harley's enormous collection of automotive tools. It was boy heaven there.

And on top of that, there was Hiram.

"Herd's drifting off to the left," Hiram said, and it was.

The eleven-year-old Walter had to get thirty head of cattle from the trampled south pasture over the creek to the southeast pasture where the undergrowth had been sprouting for two weeks now. It was the first time Harley had let him take any of the livestock from one place to another where there was no fencing along the way. Hiram rode on the air alongside Walter. He bobbed up and down as though he too was on a horse. Maybe somewhere he was.

"Calf's wandering and its mother's going off to get it," Walter agreed. "If they don't get back with the herd by the time they're in the water I'll round them up."

"Bad timing," Hiram said. "They're not going to

make a decision to step into the water if you don't make them. And by that time there'll be more of them wandering out downstream. They won't stampede or nothing, but they'll be out of control."

"I'm getting the main body down the hill to the creek like Dad said. They're all branded. If I can't get them back until later what else can I do?"

"There's a lot you can do that you don't know about," the ghost said. He looked thoughtfully at the boy. "Hold out your left hand."

He did.

"Now flick the nail of your middle finger with your thumbnail and watch it."

A tiny spark of light came off the middle finger and a small electrical arc flashed between his two fingers for a little longer than a second.

"Yeah," Walter said, "so what?"

"Do you know what that is?"

"My dad told me some weird things would start happening with my body," Walter told the ghost as though he knew everything in the world that anybody could know. "It has to do with puberty."

The ghost slapped himself across the face. Walter could see through where he slapped himself on the face. The ectoplasm, or whatever it was, parted at his cheek, through which Walter could see a steer shove a cow over on her side to splash in the creek.

"What?" Walter said.

"Do you think everybody can make sparks with their fingertips?" Hiram wanted to know.

"No," Walter thought, "just kids starting puberty. It's like when hair starts com—"

Hiram flew toward Walter's face, hovered there closer than his nose and said, "Who told you that? Your ghost-buster father who knows everything too?" Walter nearly fell off the back of his horse.

"No," Walter said. "But I figured—"

"You figured you were nothing special so everybody must be able to do that. Everybody must be able to focus electric energy from the molecules of his cells. Everybody's a walking electric eel or a firefly. Everybody can throw off enough energy in a second to light a city for a month. Everybody can get into the Internet by just thinking about it. Everybody can snatch a radio signal out of the air on the other side of the world and turn it into a short circuit. Is that what you think?"

"You don't talk about this stuff, Hiram. You're a cowhand."

"I didn't talk about this stuff when I was a cowhand, but now I'm not any more. And I've got a job to do."

"What are you talking about? What job?"

"To hang around with you and show you what your job is, that's my job. Because you can do things nobody else can do. Because you're special."

"Stop it, Hiram. I'm a kid."

"You're a kid like there's never been. Hold out that left hand toward the straying cattle, Wally."

Walter held out his hand toward the half-dozen strays. Hiram touched his ghostly hand to Walter's left wrist.

STATIS

He squeezed. Walter felt a tingling up his arm all the way down to his gut.

A narrow shoot of lightning flowed out from Walter's fingertips. It sputtered to the left of the straying cows and steers, forming into a shimmering golden fence. It lasted just long enough for most of the bovines to bump into it with their noses or their haunches and jump back with shock. They turned and wandered languidly down into the creek away from the flickering fence. Problem solved.

"Wow," Walter said. "That felt neat."

"My whole life was about dying young on this spread so I could learn enough in the next eighty-odd years to teach you what you've got to know. I've just been waiting here for you to be born. You're my reward."

"What do you mean? I'm some kind of messiah or something?"

"You wish, kid," the ghost of the old ranch hand said. "They don't send out cowpokes to nursemaid messiahs. They'd send somebody like Lincoln or P. T. Barnum to take care of that stuff."

"So who do they send out cowpokes to nursemaid?" the boy asked.

"Mutant kids is who," the ghost said, and vanished.

"Cool."

"You guys got much experience with ghosts?" Walter asked. He was wrapped in a blanket in a corner of a couch in the living room of Xavier's School for Gifted Youngsters. He shivered as he said it. He drifted in and out of pain, in and out of weakness. But he was finally here among his own kind, without secrets. It was a relief for him to find them.

"Ghosts? You gotta be kidding," Jubilee said.

"We've got ghosts all over back home," Jono said.

"Ever make friends with one?" said Walter.

"Friends with a ghost?" said Jono. "Be like making friends with a rock."

Walter shrugged, huddling under his blanket.

With the meeting over, Everett and Angelo off to Boston looking for adventure, and the room mostly emptied, Walter gave himself a few minutes on the couch to see if he could find his breath. Sean sat down near him.

"What do you know about ghosts?" Sean asked.

"I was pretty much raised by one."

"Excuse me?"

As they talked, Walter pressed his hands together, gathering an electrical force from his cells to strengthen himself. Without Sean's knowledge he also directed a probe into Sean's electrical aura.

There was an energy here, but it was not a ghost. Walter knew that as surely as he knew the difference between a poplar tree and a tulip. It was an entity of some sort, and therefore had to be linked to this place through something organic: a person. Walter felt an intelligence behind it, so it had to be using an intelligent life force to permeate the place.

No, it wasn't Sean Cassidy. His electrostatic "signature" was different.

"So you mean to tell me," Sean was saying, "that this spirit of a dead cowboy talked to you? Hung out with you? Like . . . the Canterville Ghost?"

"Excuse me?" Walter was distracted. He knew the key to the problem was not Sean.

"The Canterville Ghost. An old story about a cowardly ghost who convinces a descendent to act brave on his behalf so he can go to heaven."

"Heaven, huh?"

Sean thought he had stepped into a *faux pas*. The boy was dying, after all. Sean's mind just wouldn't kick into gear, and he suddenly felt the need to be somewhere else. "Oh. Nothing. Sorry. Got to go check my e-mail. Waiting for a message from Hank."

Walter nodded. He had met Hank McCoy, aka the Beast, weeks earlier. McCoy had examined Walter and verified that he was dying.

"We'll talk later," and Sean was up the stairs and in his office.

This is actually kind of interesting, Walter thought. People were being indulgent of him because he was dying. It made him feel more powerful than his power did.

He arose from the sofa and slowly walked outside. He saw Jubilee heading toward the biosphere. "Want to see it?" she asked Walter.

"Sure." Snow melted onto the walkway.

He reached around her aura. All wrong. Too scattered. This entity, whatever it was, had latched onto someone focused and deep. It wasn't Jubilee.

"You should see the new holographic wall

projections," she gushed. "They're to die for."

Walter suppressed a smile and managed to look a little pained instead.

"Oh I'm sorry," Jubilee said.

"For what?" he asked.

"For . . . for nothing. Nothing at all. You want to see this?"

"Maybe later."

"Sure thing," and Jubilee was inside the biosphere and out of sight.

Walter turned and saw Chamber skulking under a tree out by the edge of the woods. He sat there with an open book—*The Leviathan* by Thomas Hobbes—and certainly ignoring it. Instead, he focused on Monet and Paige doing gymnastics routines: Paige on a setup of uneven bars on a macadam, and Monet about forty feet up in the sky, matching Paige move for move. And Jono watched.

"Not bad, huh?" Walter sat down next to Jono.

"Nasty, brutish, and short," Jono said, his eyes clearly fixed on Monet and Paige.

"'Scuse?"

"Life in the state of nature," Jono said, waving the unread book in Walter's face, "according to Thomas Hobbes. Nasty, brutish, and short."

"Hobbes himself was nasty, brutish, and short as I recall," Walter said.

"He was that. Nobody you'd want to share a bus seat with. Don't tell me you've read Hobbes?"

"What? You think they don't have libraries in Nebraska? A friend of mine told me it might be important for me to read, so I did.'' Walter liked this Chamber character. He was the only one who did not seem intimidated by Walter's medical status.

"What do you think?"

"I think those are two real good-looking girls."

"Oh them?" Jono snorted. "Hadn't noticed."

"Really?"

"Yeah," Chamber said casually. "When you see them day in and day out and waking up in the morning and coming out of the shower, you start thinking of them in a kind of sisterly way."

"Hmm," Walter said, and sat quietly for a bit.

Paige swung up into the sky above the higher bar. She twisted twice, spinning counter-clockwise as she somersaulted and caught the lower bar, flipping over it once, twice, three times. Then she snatched the higher bar again with her feet and continued her routine. Monet did exactly the same thing a fraction of a second behind, hovering high in the sky on an imaginary pair of bars. "So did you go to Catholic school?" Walter asked Chamber.

"No, I—" Jono paused and if he had a mouth he would have smiled. "Was always rather fond of the sisters, though."

Statis chuckled and gave his new friend Chamber an affectionate tap on the shoulder. Maybe the Scotsman felt the little electrical arc that encased him for just the moment he was touched by the young Nebraskan.

Maybe he didn't. Jono was not the one Walter was looking for.

Paige, Walter thought. *Wow, Paige. Now there's a girl who's focused.* She finished up on the uneven bars. *Will you look at that? Pegged that landing but good.* Up in the sky Monet made the same move, arched her back, bowed to an imaginary cheering crowd, and flew off into the clouds to who-knew-where.

Walter approached Paige as she began stretching and running in place to keep her heart rate up. "Is that what they mean by *homo superior*?" he asked her.

"It's what they call hard work, Farmboy," Paige said with a smile.

He snapped his fingers together, aware of Jono, hunkered under his tree pretending to read Hobbes, studying the two of them talking. No matter. He just wanted to see . . .

. . . *wow! What an aura!*

Not the right one, though. Too bad.

"I'm sorry about your illness, Walter," Paige said as he turned to leave.

"Thank you. I am too."

"It's hard for these guys to talk about it. We've all lost so many people."

"Well this'll be easier. You know from the top that you're going to lose me."

"How can you be so . . . so . . ."

"Flip? I don't know. It's kind of a game now. I've said my good-byes to my family, to everybody I've ever loved," Walter said and added, "so far."

"Well, if it gets too much and you want to talk about it," Paige said, taking the towel back from him, "let me know."

He thanked her and walked away. He had to scan the others before he could rest. The electricity was distinct and getting stronger.

Life in the state of mutancy: nasty, brutish and short.

Emma Frost, the White Queen, sat on the rail of a gazebo at the edge of the property where the river ran off to the south. Walter had read about her. Everybody had read about her. World-famous industrialist at a very young age. Also found time to run a snooty New England private school—this place, back when it was just the Massachusetts Academy. It wasn't until he met Sean that Walter found out that she was also a telepath.

Now here was a woman who knew about loss, he knew.

"Hello, Walter," she said without turning around.

This took him aback. Sean had told him that she was unable to get through the web of electrostatic energy that guarded his mind.

"How'd you know it was me?"

"You're the only one it could have been," she said with a sad smile. "You're the only one whose mind doesn't have my footprints all over it."

A sad smile, but a beautiful smile. Yet here she was feeling sorry for him, just like the others. This disappointed him.

"What can I do for you, Statis?"

"Nothing much. Tell me about my adopted home if you like."

"Your adopted home," she let out a long breath. "It's nice here if you like winter nine months a year. The snow comes. Then more snow comes. And it stays. Then it gets crunchy and dogs from the neighbors' homes go running through it because they're light enough to stay on the surface. When the dogs find a deer they scare it into running. The first step it takes over the crust, it falls in up to its ankles so it's stuck long enough for the dogs to rip it apart. The weather makes house pets into predators. Then the rain starts. The spring is nice, but it's short. It's the week or two between mud and flies. Have you been here for mud season? Starts today. Look at how fast the river is moving. The runoff wets everything down and even the pavement seems soft and mushy. It's a breeding ground for blackflies and mosquitoes. They say that the—"

"Excuse me? Ms. Frost?"

Emma looked up, squeezed the bridge of her nose. "I'm sorry, Walter," she said, "I guess I was thinking out loud." Another sad smile. "Jubilee would say 'It's a telepath thing.' "

"Right." *This is refreshing*, Walter thought. She was not really feeling sorry for him at all. She was feeling sorry for herself.

He reached around her with his art, his electrostatic fingers, and felt for her aura. But he couldn't find it.

That was impossible. Everyone has an electrostatic arc—human, mutant, animal, or plant—unless they've been dead for years. Clearly, if Emma Frost was dead, it was a very recent development.

Then he realized his error: He could not distinguish her aura from the one that electrified the air all over this place. It was such a perfect match that Walter could not tell where Emma's aura ended and the tremors in the air began.

For the first time, Emma "heard" something from Walter that he did not actually speak out loud. *You're the one*, his mind told her through all the static hissing, distorted but quite understandable.

"Which one?" she asked him out loud.

"I—Did I say something?"

She turned to face him. "You said, 'You're the one,' didn't you?"

"I . . . must have," he said, perplexed. "I have to go see Mr. Cassidy."

"His door is always open. He's probably already told you that."

"Yes."

"Would you like me to come with you?"

"I don't know. I guess it would be helpful." He wanted to avoid her, but at the same time keep an eye on her.

"Well then I'll be along, I suppose," she said, not budging from her perch overlooking the raging Mad River.

"Ms. Frost?"

"Yes?"

GENERATION X

"You're thinking about the Hellions, aren't you?"
"I am. And do you read minds too, Walter?"
"Not often."
"You go ahead. I'll be along."

CHAPTER SIX

THE FORMER GAZEBO

"**W**hat you're saying is full of speculation and hocus-pocus, Walter," Banshee shook his head. He got up from behind his desk and paced back and forth, narrowly avoiding the computer books that littered his floor. Walter followed him with his eyes as if watching a Ping-Pong match. "Electrical auras and individual signatures?"

"You can fly and have a sonic scream. Chamber doesn't have a face. Skin has too much of one. Ms. Frost can read minds," Walter said. "How's this more outlandish?"

"I didn't say it was outlandish," Sean said defensively. "In fact, it's as good an explanation as I've heard. I just don't know whether it's good enough to act on."

Sean stopped pacing and held his temples. Was this the decisive, fast-on-his-feet mentor of the next generation of X-Men? Somehow, Walter didn't think so.

"I mean the other day I couldn't figure out why I was so glum," Sean said, almost to himself, "so I got on the net and spent money. Made me feel better for a while but then the next morning I was down again and it seemed so was everybody else. Everybody was running off some mood or drowning some sorrow or howling at the moon in the middle of the day and all I could do to deal with it was call meetings where everybody fed off everybody else's depression."

Walter was staring at Sean, trying to figure out what he was talking about.

"Except you," the headmaster added. "And you're . . ."

"Dying?" Walter prompted.

"Yeah. Are you taking anti-depressants or pain-killers or something? You know we can't have controlled substances around—"

"No, Mr. Cassidy, no drugs."

"That's the sort of thing that'll bring the authorities down around our necks. They'll come with dogs and helicopters. Probably this time of year, too, because the tourists are all going off to—"

"Mr. Cassidy? Excuse me?"

"What?"

"You're running at the mouth, sir," Walter said. "A lot like Ms. Frost was just a few minutes ago out at the gazebo, if you don't mind my saying, sir."

"No." Sean paused, then picked up speed again. "No, I don't mind. If I minded I'd say so for sure because I speak my mind. That's why I've come to get along so much better with Emma. When we first started working here we—"

"Mr. Cassidy—"

"What?"

"Mr. Cassidy, I really don't have much time. I am dying and all."

Sean stared at Walter. Then Walter laughed to let Sean know he meant it as a joke.

"A little black humor there," Sean said, and allowed a small laugh of his own.

"Look, Mr. Cassidy. There's something going on

here. And so far it's affected the two most responsible people in the place the most.''

''That would be Emma and me.''

Walter put a finger to his forehead in some consternation—but no, he would not give in to it. ''Yeah. That's right. Come with me, maybe we can figure this out.''

''What is it exactly that we're figuring out?''

''I'll show you when we get there,'' Walter said, and actually took Sean by the arm and began to lead him gingerly out the office door. ''What kind of mechanical diagnostic equipment have you got in the garage?''

This is coming along quite well, the consciousness decided. The female Frost was under control. The others were coming along. The only significant impediments were the flawed one and the damaged one. The consciousness would inflame that flaw and let the damage take care of itself.

The old carriage house that now served as the school's garage and machine shop was chock full of the coolest cars Walter had ever seen in one place. Besides the five remaining Jeeps that seemed to be the only things anyone ever drove, there was a Ferrari from the eighties, a Mazerati from the seventies, an Aston Martin from the sixties, and a Lotus from the fifties. Anything older than that—and there were another half-dozen that had to be older than that—were cars even Walter did not recognize. Oh, there was a Stutz Bearcat—he'd never seen one of those except in pictures—and an old Reo. *Is that a Stanley Steamer? No, it couldn't be. Well, what else could it be?*

"Ever need any help fixing these babies up?" Walter asked Sean.

"Yeah," Sean said. "There's this kid, Timmy Murdock, works in a filling station down the road. His dad runs one of the ski areas. Mechanical acumen like Nicola Tesla himself."

"Tall thin kid? Lots of freckles? Built like a runner or a bike rider?"

"That's the one. Met him?"

"Never heard of him."

"Thought of checking to see if he's a mutant, but I'd be afraid to find out he was one of us."

"Why?"

"If we made a super hero out of him he might let my cars go to seed."

"Good point."

While the pair talked, Walter sludged through the workshop gathering up what seemed to be disparate pieces of old electronic gadgets: an oscilloscope, a voltmeter, a length of telephone wire, a defunct Packard Bell laser printer whose only working part seemed to be the fuser, heart pads that looked like some nightmare device out of *Flatliners*, some arcane hand tools. It was boy heaven in here. Walter considered moving in.

He sat down and began disassembling the printer.

Sean left Walter alone with the toys that only a young Victor Frankenstein could love.

Hours later, he returned to check on his newest student's progress.

Walter held up a Rube Goldberg-esque collection of pieced-together artifacts that looked as though they could do nothing more useful than hang in the Guggenheim.

"What do you call it?"

"I've got to give it a name?" Walter asked.

"Well, it would help the rest of us that have to believe whatever data it gives us."

"Oh." Walter flipped on a hanging switch he had cannibalized from the laser printer. He rubbed his charged hand over one of the chest pads, creating sparks. With his other hand he held up the other pad, pointing it at Sean. A hazy green light outlined an image approximating Sean's figure on the screen. "I call it Hiram."

"Hiram."

"And that's your Kirlian aura."

"Really? Mine?"

"Yeah," the boy said, "now let me go show you Ms. Frost's."

Emma read Sartre as she sat empty-handed on the gazebo. Somewhere about fifteen miles to the northeast in the enormous library of the University of Massachusetts at Amherst, a rather emotionally unattractive and depressed young undergraduate named Carla DeMoffrey was reading a book by Jean-Paul Sartre called *Nausea*. It was roughly as depressing as its title and Emma found comfort in the girl's distant thoughts as she read through Carla's mind.

Sean interrupted Emma and her sudden exit from Carla's brain made the UMass student hiccup, but she continued reading. Emma thought, *Now the girl would get ahead of me and I'll have to find an actual hard copy of the bloody thing.*

"What do you want?" she asked Sean.

"Just for you to sit still for a moment," he said, smiling. He and Walter carried various components of the weird electronic puddingstone that the boy had rigged together. Walter rubbed his hand now on one of the chest pads.

"Sitting still is what I was doing in the first place," she snapped. "Maybe I can pick up without losing more than a paragraph or two," and off she was in apparent reverie again, searching through the faraway carrels for Carla DeMoffrey's concave consciousness.

"There. See?" Walter said as the screen filled with green light and the gadget hummed with static.

"What am I seeing?" Sean asked.

"There's just that little figure of Ms. Frost's body in the center and the aura fills the rest of the screen. No matter how far back we walk, the aura's all over the place, and it's depressing the bejeebers out of everyone here. You know that yourself."

"How do I know that?"

"Look," Walter tried to explain as if he were talking

to a three-year-old, "no one gives off an aura that big. Hell, Einstein himself would at least have had breaks in the aura if we stood this close to him. But walk backward and no matter how far back you go, as long as we train this pad on Ms. Frost, the aura will still fill the screen. There's some outside force merging with her aura and it's doing something weird to the school and everyone in it."

Sean paused, assimilating. "And how do we know this?"

Now Walter paused. "I thought I . . ." and he could not find a way to explain it any more clearly. "Mr. Cassidy, Ms. Frost is the carrier of some sort of malevolent force that's making us act crazy. There's something bad brewing and we're just sitting here letting it."

"Oh," Sean said.

Quite suddenly, the gazebo Emma sat on buckled with the rattling of the earth below it, and flew upward in two pieces, hurling Emma up into the air with it.

On a reflex, Sean was off the ground into the sky.

Emma tumbled through the air in a meteor swarm of wooden and rock debris. She was thirty feet in the air and rising before she realized, again falling out of touch with her remote Sartre fan, that she was in trouble. She was wondering whether she cared when Sean snatched her into his arms and flew her out over the river away from the falling shards of former gazebo.

As Walter stood, eyes widening, a spit of fire rose from the crater that the newly airborne belvedere created. From the fire stepped a tall, thickset boy. Statis shot a charge of electricity to surround the advancing figure but it had no effect. The boy was an illusion.

"Beef!" Emma howled from the relative safety of Sean's arms. Together, they descended.

The debris clattered to the ground. The swell of Earth receded. The fire died. And the image of the big young man faded.

"You saw him too?" she demanded of Walter.

"Yes."

"So what do you think now?" Sean asked him.

"There's something else here," Walter replied.

"Right," Emma said, kicking up a pile of wooden slats. "Do we have a copy of *Nausea* in the library, Sean?" she asked as she walked away.

"What?" he said, and then forgot the question.

CHAPTER SEVEN
THE HAYMARKET

Boston was a great place to be a kid. It was one of those towns that was big enough to have an honest-to-goodness skyline and small enough to walk from one end of it to the other in an afternoon. And it was full of colleges: Harvard and MIT, full of rich, anxiety-ridden suburban kids who wanted to grow up to win Nobel Prizes. Tufts and Brandeis, full of rich, anxiety-ridden kids who didn't make it into Harvard or MIT. Boston University, Boston College, and Northeastern University whose students were just as smart as those at the hotter schools but whose anxiety levels were lower. Then there were all the real colleges where the real kids went who were going to grow up to hire the kids from the hot colleges: UMass. Babson. Simmons. Emerson. Bentley. Bradford. Berklee School of Music and Boston Conservatory. There were junior colleges all over the place. Dozens of them. All crawling with babes.

"Okay," Everett told Angelo, "you know what's the first thing I want to do?" as they walked out of the garage under Boston Common where they'd parked the Jeep.

Angelo looked around, rubbing his hands together and drinking in the smells and the scenery. "I can't even guess," he said.

"I want to walk the Freedom Trail," Everett said.

Angelo stopped short. Screwed up his forehead in knots and slitted his eyes. His face with its overloose skin looked like hotel bedsheets the way the chambermaid found them in the morning.

THE HAYMARKET

After a moment Everett realized he was walking up Tremont Street by himself. He turned around and went back to see what was wrong with Angelo.

"What did you say?"

"I want to walk the Freedom Trail," Everett said again.

"Wait a minute." Angelo pulled back the skin of his face so that he looked more like a human and less like a Chinese hunting dog. "You're standing here, with your main man—me—in one of the major babe towns of the Western Hemisphere, with no discernible adult supervision, a walletful of cash, reasonably good looks, your whole life ahead of you, and *super-powers* for heaven's sakes, and you want to go off and have a history lesson?"

"Well I didn't think of it that way."

"Exactly what way did you think of it?"

Now Everett screwed up his face. "I think I've never been in Boston before without Sean or a bunch of guys who wanted to just find someplace to eat or to hunt down some big super-villain menace to the planet. I've always heard about the Freedom Trail and I never got a chance to walk it. The Old North Church. Old Ironsides. The Old Corner Bookstore. Get it?"

"I'm getting old real fast." Angelo looked his friend up and down. "You're not going on the Freedom Trail."

"Why not?"

"You're going to be too busy fighting off the girls."

"Where? What girls?"

"Look around you, Synch. Tall girls. Short girls. Skinny girls. Zaftig girls."

"Zaftig girls?"

"Zaftig. It's a *barrio* word," Angelo said. "You wouldn't know. How do you like your girls? Sweet and black like your coffee?"

"I like them . . . I like them like . . ."

"You don't know, do you?"

"I know. I know. I like them friendly."

"Now you're talking, pal," Angelo resumed their walk up Tremont at a rabid clip. "Now you're talking."

"So where're we going to find these friendly girls?"

Angelo looked around, confused for a moment. He then waved his long arms in the air and gestured expansively, the tips of his fingers flapping in the breeze.

Everett looked at Skin dubiously.

"Wait," Angelo said. "Wait. Watch this." He went trotting up to a bevy of half-a-dozen young women carrying their cool up the street. "Excuse me, ladies."

They walked. Angelo walked backward in front of them.

"Excuse me, but my friend Everett and I—Everett, smile for the ladies—" one sweet young thing looked at Synch's smile and seemed a little impressed but kept walking anyway "—Everett and I are strangers in town and wonder where we might best find some good food and good company."

They walked. Maybe a little more briskly but with no less cool.

"Everett, why don't you show these nice people how

you can lift them up off the ground using your mind? John Travolta's got nothing on this dude.''

Synch didn't bite.

''Really, ladies. Where do a couple of likely young men like us go to slack off? To loosen up? To make friends?''

The young women walked on. And as they walked, one of them—a statuesque college kid with long red hair and a cello case—turned without breaking her stride and said, ''Why don't you try Sporter's, boys?'' and the other young women all giggled and walked on and away.

''You don't know any more about finding girls than I do, do you?'' Everett grinned that put-'em-away-before-they-know-what-hit-'em grin.

''What are you talking about? You heard the lady. Why don't we just look up this 'Sporter's' place in the phone book?''

''Why don't we just do it my way? Look.'' They reached the corner of the Common and Everett pointed up Park Street. ''We can start over there at the State House.''

The State House was the starting point, not for the Freedom Trail, but for a recently minted historical walking tour called ''The Black Heritage Trail.'' Everett had been particularly anxious to see this.

''Look at this, Skin,'' Everett called, waving his hands as his pal lagged behind. ''It's the Fifty-Fourth Regiment Memorial! The first black infantry unit in the Civil War. Remember *Glory*? Denzel Washington won an Oscar. We lost the battle but we won the war.'' Everett was beside himself with the excitement of his discovery.

"Ding ding for our side," Angelo waved a flapping forefinger in circles in the air.

In the early days of the nineteenth century—when English and Arab slave traders were still dropping boatloads of kidnapped Africans onto the docks of Charleston and Annapolis and New Orleans like so many striped bass—a prominent black preacher from New Hampshire named Thomas Paul came to Boston to found the First African Baptist Church. Black people were allowed to attend white churches in Boston in those days, as long as they sat up in the balconies and did not try to speak or vote at congregational meetings.

For a little over a year, Preacher Paul led worship services at Faneuil Hall, a stop on the Freedom Trail. A generation earlier, the Adams boys had raised the rabble against their British overlords in that same location. Then, near the end of 1806, Preacher Paul's followers opened the spanking new African Meeting House on land that the black Baptist congregation had bought in a little cul-de-sac off Joy Street near Smith Court. At the dedication ceremony, attended and celebrated by the crème de Boston's crème, there were only the crèmey faces of white officials and abolitionists allowed in the floor-level pews while the members of the congregation huddled in their own balcony and craned to see Thomas

Paul sitting behind the pulpit and listening to the mayor speak.

Nearly two hundred years later, with his friend Angelo tapping a foot impatiently at the doorway, a young black mutant from St. Louis vaulted over the cloth barrier that still attempted to keep history buffs of all races, creeds, colors, and genetic conditions off the merchandise. He plopped himself down in a high-backed chair behind the pulpit and extended his aura of synchronicity to "grab" the voice box of his best friend across the room.

Against his will, Angelo straightened up his spine as though someone had run a broomstick up it and declaimed to the empty hall: "And now, speaking for the opposition, the honorable Everett Thomas."

"Thank you, thank you," Everett began, "you're all too kind. Please sit down. Oh please, save your applause for my sterling oratory."

Angelo yanked back his body into his own control. "Hey when'd you learn to do that, Brother?"

"Something I figured out in a tutoring session with Emma."

"Geez, I better pay more attention in class."

"No heckling, sir. I stand before you today," Everett said to the world at large, "because I can't fit behind you."

Angelo buried his face in his hand. Then he loosened some more skin so he could pretty much bury his whole head in it like an ostrich.

"I come bringing news from the west where the sun sets later and the winter lasts forever."

"Boy, are you lucky no one but me is listening to you, clown boy."

"There comes a time in every man's life when he must take a stand. Pro or con. For or against. With 'em or agin' 'em. This is such a time."

"You have the most extraordinary speaking voice." It was an unexpected sound from the shadows in the back of the big meeting hall. With that a pair of stunningly beautiful young women, one black and one Asian, stepped into the light near the rearmost pews. "Deep and round, like a young James Earl Jones," it was the black woman, tall and—what did Skin call it? *zaftig*?—with shiny hair that framed her face in curls, talking to Everett, "though it would be so much more impressive if you had something to say."

Everett said, "Uhh."

"I'm LaWanda," she said, "and this is my friend Amanda."

Amanda smiled and said, "Hi."

Everett said, "Uhh."

Angelo sucked himself together, looked himself over to be sure nothing was hanging out that shouldn't be, and stepped up to say, "I'm Angelo and this is my friend Everett. Would you ladies like to go for a cup of coffee or something?"

"Love to," Amanda said.

"Sure," LaWanda said.

Everett said, "Uhh."

THE HAYMARKET

*　　*　　*

They were both in their first year at Lasell Junior College a few miles out of the city proper in a little suburb called Auburndale. LaWanda was from a well-to-do family on the north shore of Long Island and she was majoring—so far—in art history. Amanda's parents were Vietnamese refugees who moved to northern California a few years before Amanda was born. At her father's insistence, Amanda was a business major but her real passion, she told Angelo, was gymnastics.

Gymnastics, Angelo thought. Now there was something he could talk to her about. When he knew her better.

The four sat at a table, gulping down coffee and hot chocolate in the noisy main foyer of Quincy Market at Haymarket Square, a short walk from Boston Harbor. This huge ancient building had no interior walls, and was full of shops and restaurants and vending stands. Predating the American Revolution, it was quite possibly the oldest shopping mall in the world.

When Amanda and LaWanda went off to the women's room, Everett said, "We'd better lay off the mutant stuff for now, don't you think, Skin?"

"Yeah, you gave me that nudge when I was going to say what school we went to. I thought you just didn't want to tell them we were younger than they are."

"No no no," Everett waved his hands. "I mean you never know how people will react."

In a moment the two young women returned, sitting next to them, giggling against their will, having apparently decided that Amanda was with Angelo and LaWanda was with Everett.

"So what are you two doing for dinner?" asked Angelo.

"Are you asking us both out?" Amanda asked and LaWanda giggled.

Everett said, "Uhh." Angelo thought, *My friend, you ought to thank your lucky stars that you're so good-looking, because if you had to get along on personality alone, you'd be in deep trouble.*

But Everett actually managed a sentence. "Have you guys ever been to Durgin Park? I haven't."

"Really?" LaWanda said as now Amanda giggled. "It's my favorite place in town. We've got to go."

There was a line to get into the three-hundred-year-old restaurant that had stood on the cobblestones of Haymarket Square since "before you were born," according to the menu. This gave Angelo a chance to put his arm around Amanda's waist and gave LaWanda a chance to take Everett's hand and make believe Everett had taken hers.

Late Sunday night, at Xavier's School for Gifted Youngsters, Walter Nowland was pacing across the living room as his new teachers and remaining fellow students draped themselves lethargically over their seats. They tried to concentrate on what he had to say.

"I'm sick, get it?"

Walter looked around at half-a-dozen blank faces, coughed hard, and swallowed.

THE HAYMARKET

"I did my mourning and my good-bye-saying back home and came here to live with my—" he almost said "my own kind," but that would have blown it "—with a community of people who might understand me. My family was great, don't get me wrong, but the folks in town didn't really. . . . Well, I came here to live with you. I'm not interested in dying with you, I'll do that alone if you don't mind. Am I getting through here?"

Sean nodded blankly, dutifully. He was not listening.

"I'm talking about what makes this place special. About what made me decide to come here. Not so much that you guys were like me, but because this was the only school left that I knew of that still taught that personal involvement was a good thing."

Monet sighed. She had planned to take herself out in East Barrington tonight to see the new Brad Pitt film. She knew this meeting was important, but she really really wanted to see that movie.

"I don't know. Maybe there's some deep dark intelligence sucking your initiative out of you. Well that's a helluva tactic if you can pull it off. All I know is that there's some weird stuff going on with auras around here. But I haven't got a clue about why it isn't doing anything to me or how to deal with it. But I bet you do, and you're not thinking."

Jubilee didn't like just being able to make fireworks with her hands. Everyone else around here could do something big and snooty like fly or take out a tank with their brain pans. It didn't have anything to do with what was going on here at this meeting—whatever was going on here at this meeting—but it was bothering her just now.

"Well you've got to work on it," Walter raised his voice, waved around his arms and those tattoos that Paige had found so enthralling yesterday, but today she didn't remember why. "Because . . . because . . . because if you don't, no one else will."

Penance was under the house. She could go where she wanted and nothing in her way stayed in the way if she didn't want it there. She hung out there often when there was a meeting, just to make sure these people who seemed to care about her did not go anywhere. Just now she was not trusting them very much.

"We are the future. Like it or not. Whatever we become is what the future becomes. Get it? Listen to me."

Emma muttered to herself about nothing in particular.

"First thing I figured out about you guys is that you're all big movie fans, aren't you?" No response, but Walter went on as if there had been a positive one. "Remember the end of *Blade Runner*? Batty, the big bad replicant, is dying, see? Like I am. We had that in common."

Paige was positively livid that Walter was dying. She felt somehow cheated that he was so well-adjusted about that condition. She had left a depressing book by Dr. Elisabeth Kübler-Ross in his room for him to read. Then she gave him some chocolates she had found at a little shop in Snow Valley. When she was in town she had found an even more depressing book by Rabbi Harold Kushner, and she gave that to him too. She wanted to talk to him, but she would have to content herself with trying to depress him for now.

"And he gives Deckard, the Harrison Ford character, this speech about all the things he's done and all the stuff he's seen and how unfair it all is. I memorized it. Thought I might use it at my funeral." That was a joke. No one noticed except Chamber, who sneered, but in a good way.

Only Jono was paying attention. He was dark and depressed as a lifestyle choice, so this overweening malaise that seemed to permeate the school compound was nothing he particularly noticed. Certainly it did not debilitate him. He was agreeing with most of what Walter was saying, and it bothered him just a little bit more than usual when he noticed that Paige did not seem involved with the meeting.

Walter closed his eyes and quoted: " 'I've seen things you people wouldn't believe. Attack ships on fire off the shoulder of Orion. I watched C-beams glitter in the dark near the Tannhauser gate. All those moments will be lost in time, like tears in rain . . .' "

Walter pinched his eyes shut and tried to focus. He seemed to reel for a moment, then recovered.

" ' . . . Time to die.' " And Walter grabbed his throat and fell on the floor in a heap. Then he started convulsing.

Jono leapt to his feet and tore a strip of gauze bandage off his own camouflage to stuff into Walter's mouth to keep him from biting down on his tongue. Monet slowly turned her head and asked absently, "What's he do-ing?"

"Somebody call the doc!" Jono demanded of his small uninvolved audience. "Paige! Sean! Somebody! Pick up the phone!" he hollered as he held Walter's head still between both palms on his lap cross-legged on the floor.

"Excuse me?" asked Sean.

"The doctor. Call the doctor. This is an emergency."

Paige raised the receiver of the phone on an end table and tapped in nine-one-one before Jonothon crooked Walter's head in an elbow of one arm and reached the other hand over to slap down the receiver button.

"Not the bleedin' cops, for bleedin' sakes!" he spit out. "Someone hold down his legs. Help me, will you? What's Dr. McCoy's pager number? Banshee, the Beast's pager, do you know it?"

"Oh, Hank. Sure," Sean said. "Umm, it's zero on the autodialer."

Jono yanked the phone over to himself by the wire, punched MEMORY and 0. An operator came on. Jono pressed a little black button in the handle of the receiver and a rather good computer simulation of what he had to say made its way from the sonic sound waves of Chamber's midsection into the operator's ear. This house was the only place on Earth, as far as Jonothon knew, where he could actually pick up a telephone, "talk" on it, and have the person at the other end hear what he had to say. Jono had heard recordings of the voice that the school's phones claimed was his. "Sounds like the robot on bleedin' *Lost in Space*," he had complained to Paige, who had giggled.

Jono told the operator who answered that the message was, "Medical emergency, Snow Valley," and before he was off the line an operator from the Massachusetts State Police broke in to ask why someone had dialed 911 and then hung up. For all Jono's frantic calm in trying to explain that the number was misdialed and there was nothing to concern the police, the operator still said she would dispatch someone to check up on the place in the next few minutes. It was the unnaturally hollow quality of Jono's "voice" that simply refused to inspire confidence over the phone. "I'd advise you to have the gate open when the unit gets there," the operator said and hung up.

Grasshoppers mutate into locusts when there is too little food in too little space, and they swarm over the land, eating until there is nothing left. Sometimes the patrons of Durgin Park were a lot like those grasshoppers. Fortunately, the staff served plenty of food. Everyone sat on benches at long narrow tables with big silver pitchers of ice water and plateloads of corn bread. The smells of the kitchen whipped your olfactories up to a swarming frenzy. The waitresses, most of whom had worked there since the restaurant's founding—no matter what the menu claimed—were big and rude and took it as a matter of duty to keep the clientele in line. This restaurant was established to cater to the dockworkers and sailors who were the dominant lifeform in this corner of the city before the tourists started overwhelming the place.

One day, not long before Christmas of 1773, Samuel Adams and a few of his rowdy friends came to Durgin Park to drink a few bucketloads of ale and fill themselves up on turkey and prime rib. Before Sam's gang left the place, they put on war paint and Indian feathers, then went down to the docks to unload three shipsful of King George's overpriced tea and drop it into the harbor.

The crew of rude gargantuan waitresses at Durgin Park that night may not actually have been the same women in charge of the dining room the night Skin and Synch were there with their dates, but they may as well have been.

After a meal worthy of dodging surly waitresses, the four kids prepared to leave.

"You're sorry?" a voice boomed from the far corner of the dining room. "You can't spill my food in my lap and get off by just saying you're sorry!" A beefy black man in his twenties, wearing an expensive suit, argued with a Korean kid who sported an attitude and a T-shirt that said NO FEAR.

"I said sorry," the T-shirt snapped. "What else you want, I should lick the bread crumbs off your lap?"

Angelo stepped away from Amanda but Everett put a hand on his arm. *No need, friend*, the hand said.

It didn't go much further. Four waitresses grabbed the two men in half-nelsons and garnered the applause of most of the seated diners. The waitresses shoved the two past Synch, Skin, and their new friends, down the stairs, and out the door. In theory, they would look at each other, snort and huff a little, and go home.

In reality, Everett, LaWanda, Angelo, and Amanda, hoping to find a shortcut to the Square, found the two food-fighters were pummelling each other with fists.

"Get out of here," Everett told both girls. "Meet us back at the restaurant."

They nodded and hurriedly walked away.

Meanwhile, Angelo maneuvered behind the expensive suit and tapped him on the shoulder. As the man turned, Skin snaked a frond of flesh around his ankles and tripped him up.

At the same time, the T-shirt reeled his arm back for a punch. Skin shot out a tentacle of flesh. It wrapped around the younger man's arm and fist, yanking him down to the ground.

By the time Synch came into the skirmish, it was already over. The fight had been more fair than when the enemy was a quartet of huge pre-colonial-era waitresses.

"Reel in the skin, Skin," Everett whispered. "No need to show anyone our tricks."

"Do your stuff," Angelo said as he retracted his flesh.

"Who the hell do you guys think you are?" the T-shirt demanded.

Everett smiled and extended his synchronicity aura to the expensive suit's digestive tract. "Yeah, you think you can step in between—" and the man's esophagus, just above his stomach, squished inward "—two starving . . . really hungry . . . oh . . ."

The would-be street fighter surrendered what was left

of his lunch on the bricked sidewalk and his expensive-looking Italian shoes.

As the T-shirt raised a hand to point and ridicule, the synchronicity aura shifted. "You tossed it in public, you—" then Everett's control wrapped around his voice box, "—poor guy. I didn't mean to cause you this distress."

The other one who had gone to his knees, suddenly recovered, looked up and said, "I feel much better now. I'm sorry too."

Everett relaxed his hold on both of them. Perplexed only for a moment, the one helped the other to his feet. There would be no fight after all. Everett and Angelo walked back to the restaurant with a spring in their steps.

When they met back up with the girls, LaWanda immediately asked, "Did they kill each other?"

"Nah," said Everett, "we talked them out of fighting. They weren't bad guys. Just out of sorts."

Angelo shrugged. "We reasoned with them. They listened to our infectious optimism and goodwill."

Everett high-fived Angelo and both of them realized what a strain that little secret interchange with superpowers was. Instead of walking around, they walked back to the Jeep Wrangler. They took the number of Amanda and LaWanda's dorm phones, gave them a ride up Commonwealth Avenue to Lasell and promised to call in the morning. Angelo kissed Amanda on the hand. That was what you did on first dates, he had told Everett long ago, they love it. Everett remembered too late. No matter, they were here for a week.

THE HAYMARKET

The moment the girls were out of sight, Angelo let go and his skin flopped all over the passenger seat.

"So what's the deal, bro'?" Everett asked, pulling out of the main campus parking lot. "The penalty for having a nice evening is having to watch you decompress?"

"Yeah, man," Angelo hissed through a foot-and-a-half of drooping lips, "I didn't know how long you were going to make me keep up appearances. Pretty gross, huh?"

"That was really nice," Amanda told LaWanda on the stairway up to the second floor of their dormitory.

"Yeah," LaWanda said, "*really* nice."

"I mean they treated us like ladies and didn't let us see the check and said they'd call us and didn't even hit on us."

"Oh they will. They always do."

"You really think so?"

"What? Think they'll hit on us?"

"No, call us."

LaWanda smiled. "They'll call the minute they get up in the morning."

"Really?"

"Sure."

"Hope they don't sleep too late."

Both giggled.

"Isn't the meeting tomorrow night?" Amanda asked.

"I think so," LaWanda said, looking at the bulletin board in the lounge as they came out of the stairwell. "Yeah, right here. Tomorrow at eight. Brattle Street."

"Think they'd want to come?"

"If they call. Don't see why not."

"Do you think they really will?"

"Call? Yeah."

"No. Hit on us."

"I don't know. I bet they do."

"Really? When?"

"Third date."

"Really?"

"Why?"

"What do you mean 'Why?' "

"I mean what'll you do? If Angelo hits on you?"

Amanda paused. "I don't know, but I can't wait to find out."

CHAPTER EIGHT
THE BEAST

Massachusetts State Trooper Michael Brown had finally made it through the weather a few minutes before midnight in answer to Paige Guthrie's mistaken 911 emergency call. He sat in the drive outside the main building of Xavier's School for Gifted Youngsters for a minute or two, wondering why the main dormitory building at a school for teenagers would be lit up like a Christmas tree this late at night. Then he gathered up his cop-ness, unloaded himself from the driver's seat, hung his head up high off the back of his neck, and ambled toward the main door thirty yards away.

A big man, Mike had started as a lineman for two years at UMass-Amherst and been first-string quarterback his junior year. By the end of his sophomore year he was majoring in biochemistry and running a solid three-point-four average.

Sometime during his junior year he pulled a ligament hotdogging down Bobby's Run trying to do an umbrella turn on an impossibly vertical ski run to impress some snow bunny. The snow bunny, as it turned out, was studying for a Ph.D. in women's studies at Dartmouth. Said Ph.D., by the name of Jill, felt moved to marry the smart, hunky now-ex-quarterback who eventually grew up to be an overeducated cop.

It was about Jill—pregnant now with their second child—that Trooper Mike Brown was thinking when a light poured out a side door of the building. A narrow dark figure walked out, closing the door behind. It seemed to be a dark man carrying a megawatt flashlight. The light blinded Mike for a moment; then it went out and he heard footsteps tapping toward him in the dark. A spectral unearthly voice—it seemed to come from all around him—said, "Hi."

The figure did not stand very tall. In fact, he was very slight, almost emaciated. Draped in black leather, his face was covered up to the nostrils in white gauze. Mike also couldn't see where he had put the flashlight.

"Is that an injury, son?" Mike asked.

"Uh, kind of. It's a long-term thing."

There was that voice again. It was not muffled by the bandages, it was just spooky. Hollow. Disembodied. At least that voice answered when he addressed the kid.

"I'm sorry," the big trooper said, pulling his head the tiniest bit forward on his neck. "I'm Trooper Michael Brown of the Massachusetts State Police answering an emergency call from this location. Is this the property of the Xavier Institute?"

"Yes, yes. You've got the right place, but there was no emergency call. Someone dialed that by mistake."

"I'm sure that's true, but we have to check out all emergency calls in the unlikely event that a call is cut short by a hostile or illegal act."

"Makes sense," he admitted

"I wonder if I might come in."

"I'm sure you might."

"Your name sir?"

"Jonothon Starsmore."

"And this is your residence?"

"I'm a student here."

"And that's a Scottish burr if I'm not mistaken?"

"Very good. It is indeed."

"I'm a Scotsman myself," Mike said, softening the contact a bit, "on my mother's side."

"How nice."

In the pitch dark Mike missed the edge of the flagstone path to the door and stuck a spit-shined black leather boot into a mud puddle.

"Maybe I can give you a light there." Jono would have grinned if he had a mouth.

"Please."

Jono turned away as Mike scraped his boot on the flagstone. Mike looked up when he saw a beam of light. A strong beam.

Mike reached up, thinking to take the torch from Jono's hand to get a better look at the gunk on his boot. He stopped when he realized that he was reaching toward the boy's face. The boy himself was shining. The bottom part of his face, as he held away the bandages, shone with what could only have been the flames of hell itself.

"Oh geez," the big cop said, as he tried to snatch a breath out of the air and couldn't find one.

Then he fainted dead away.

Dr. Henry P. McCoy had not gotten the emergency call at the Xavier Institute for Higher Learning in West-chester, as Jono had hoped, but in Washington, D.C. He had gotten it while doing some consulting work for Starcore. Apparently a microorganism that no one else could identify had latched onto an old satellite belonging to that solar project. By the time the crew of a Polaris submarine fished it out of the North Atlantic, it had grown into a rather impressive little colony. Starcore's analysis already indicated that the microorganism had joined the satellite in space and that the bug survived under the most unlikely of conditions.

No one, however, could determine without a doubt what harmful effects the thing might have on humans. They had kept the infested plastic hull of the satellite in an isolation chamber for two-and-a-half months before the head of Starcore, Dr. Peter Corbeau, got wind of it. An old friend of the X-Men, Corbeau's immediate reaction—after chewing out the responsible parties for over an hour—was to call in McCoy.

The immediate problem: the submarine crew that picked up the satellite had been at sea for over six months and the government was afraid to allow them to come home for fear that they might infect the general population with . . . whatever.

"You mean to say these gentlemen have been holed away somewhere in a vacuum tube under the ocean for all that time and you don't even know whether you're ever going to let them go?" McCoy asked a Starcore flunky by the name of Whitney when the latter called him.

"That is correct, sir."

"Do they know why they've been detained?"

"Negative, sir."

"What explanation have you given them?"

"Oh, a number of things. We've made up mechanical failures in other sister submarines and told them they have to take up the slack. We've led them to believe that their senior officers are testing secret new weaponry. We've invented a few wartime alerts to keep them busy."

McCoy took a breath and counted to ten. "Have any of the submariners displayed any discernible ill effects that may have been caused by an unknown bacterium?"

"Possibly, sir."

"Of what nature?"

"Widespread spontaneous nausea. Extended periods of inexplicable nervousness and sometimes violent hostility among the crew. General behavior unbecoming Naval personnel."

"Maybe the sort of thing you'd find in a crew of servicemen who're caught in close quarters too long looking at the same people every day without letup. Sort of thing you'd find in men who haven't been exposed to some mystery space virus."

"Perhaps, sir."

McCoy let out a long low huff of air over the phone line that sounded for all the world like a feral growl. Then he said, "Okay, sport, here's a freebie."

"Yes, sir?"

"The boys in the sub are fine. Let them go home."

"Well I mean . . . what do you mean, Dr. McCoy?"

"I mean you go tell my old friend Peter that Hank McCoy said to send the boys in that submarine home to their families. And tell him that after I'm satisfied that they've all had a nice home-cooked meal and a chance to kiss their kids goodnight, *then* I'll consider showing up to analyze your little space bug.''

"Sir, I'm authorized to tell you that—''

"And you can tell Dr. Corbeau that this is a non-negotiable point of our agreement. And, Dr. Corbeau being a generally sensible person, will probably nod his head and agree.''

"Sir,'' Whitney started. Then he heard the deep exhalation again, that growl, and he just said, "Yes sir.''

Seven minutes later the captain of the Polaris sub got an order to surface immediately and order his men to extended shore leave at the nearest allied port. That afternoon, thirty-two sailors debarked in Marseilles. The next morning, Dr. Henry McCoy perched in the darkness high on the scaffolding outside a hangar at the air base in Dover, Delaware watching his thirty-two sailors tumble out of the old plane into the arms of their parents and wives and children. That evening, McCoy reported to Starcore's Washington headquarters for his consulting gig.

Two days later, in the middle of a delicate chemical experiment, he looked at the message on his pager, left a note on a beaker promising to be back by mid-afternoon, commandeered a government Huey using an old-but-still-sometimes-useful Avengers ID card, and flew into a New England sleet storm.

McCoy patched into the phone line in Sean's office. Jono strained to hear above the noise of the 'copter blades. "The only place anywhere nearby I can see to set this crate down safely is in this open field at the coordinates I gave you, Jono. Over."

"I've got no idea how to translate your position into real space," Jono's simulated voice said, "but I've got someone here who might be able to figure it out."

"I'm all ears," the Beast said as Jono skittered out to the balcony to call down to his new friend.

The cop in the living room fumfered, "So you guys are all . . ."

"Tired," Jubilee finished his sentence. She sat to Walter's right as Paige sat to his left. Statis was wrapped, shivering, in a blanket, barely conscious. Paige sobbed, occasionally accompanying the light heaves of her chest with an appropriate whimper or two. Monet and Sean slept fitfully over the back of an easy chair and a couch respectively, and Emma curled on a rug in a corner, her eyes wide but showing no evidence of awareness of anything around her. "Very tired. We just had . . . exams."

Mike nodded uncertainly.

"Hey Mike!" Jonothon called from up above. "Somebody wants to talk to you."

"To me?" The big trooper got up and went for the stairs to Sean's office. "What, my captain?"

"No it's the doctor. A specialist. He's coming in by helicopter. Can you figure out where he is from his airline coordinates?"

"What're airline coordinates?"

Jono shrugged as he handed the phone to Mike.

THE BEAST

The trooper spoke with growing urgency: "Trooper Michael Brown, Doctor . . . I'm sure I could radio someone along the way to locate . . . yes, south of here . . . absolutely, Doctor . . . no sir . . . yes sir . . . I'll be on the road before you can land, Doctor."

Trooper Brown bolted out the door of the office and down the stairs, suddenly a man with a mission again. "Gotta get the doc here. Tell your boy to hang on."

"Hey Mike?" Jono called after him. The big cop had slammed the door behind him before Jono could holler, "Trooper Brown!"

Jono wondered if he should have told the officer about Dr. McCoy before they met.

McCoy paced back and forth in front of the big Huey, huddled under a long trenchcoat and a dark floppy hat. He was satisfied that the trooper had figured out his location. Along the road to Princeton, Brown had pingponged on his radio between McCoy himself and an air traffic control tower in Worcester where somebody had triangulated McCoy's probable position. From the air, McCoy had seen an old Coppertone billboard with a baby Jodie Foster in her undies. When Brown passed it they both knew he would arrive soon.

The Beast paced back and forth in the sleet, clapping his hands together and hopping up and down to keep warm. Then he heard the engine and saw the headlights weaving along the dirt path into the fairgrounds.

McCoy lumbered across the field toward the

advancing car, huddling under his coat and hat as the trooper stopped the unit and killed the headlights.

"Dr. McCoy, I presume."

"The very same," McCoy said as he opened the passenger-side door. Mike thought the doctor's voice sounded a lot more friendly and—well, cultured, now that it wasn't coming over a telephone or radio line.

The hulking figure of Dr. Henry McCoy sat down on the passenger seat and slammed the door after himself. Brown drove out of there forthwith.

"Next stop, Snow Valley," the trooper said, smiling as he picked up speed. Then he looked to his right into the smiling, blue-furred face of the Beast and immediately put the police car nose-first into a drainage ditch.

Fortunately Dr. McCoy was able to lift the front end of the Buick out of the big gully and shove it back up on the road. His ride was intact.

"What are you?" Mike whispered. The former quarterback was certainly a man with little fear, but he was still capable of surprise. The creature that stood before him was man-like without a doubt, but it was like nothing he had ever seen. The creature resembled a gargoyle, complete with fangs. Particles of ice forming on the blue fur that covered his head and hands (and, presumably, the rest of him).

"Maybe we weren't properly introduced. I'm Dr. Henry McCoy," and he extended an enormous furry clawed hand.

After a moment Mike understood. "You're *that*

THE BEAST

Henry McCoy," he said, "the biochemist. Used to be with the Avengers."

The Beast nodded, kept the claw open and extended.

Mike took the big blue hand in his own, and was startled to find it had an opposable thumb.

"I read your book on recombinant DNA. Before you revised it. In college," the cop said.

"You're pulling my leg."

"What, cops can't read? Get back in the car. You've got a really sick kid on your hands. Paws. Whatever."

"Look Banshee, I can't hang around here taking care of everybody. The news on Statis is bad enough and I've got a helicopter to return. What's wrong, man?"

Sean squinted through the morning at the Beast, who hunched over a battery of meters and dials in the infirmary, all connected by wires or tubes to various parts of Walter Nowland's body. "What do you mean?" Sean asked.

"Everybody around here is foggier than the weather, except for Chamber and the gendarme. What is it?"

"You're right," Sean said. "It's the weather."

"I didn't say—" Beast stopped himself as he became preoccupied with a cell scraping magnified under the special V-2 microscope in the infirmary that was the only instrument that fit the peculiar position of his eyes. "Hey Mike!" the Beast called out, and Trooper Brown, followed by Jono, came in from the hallway.

"Yeah, Doc?" said the trooper.

"Look in here and tell me what you see."

Mike Brown tried to look through both eyepieces of the microscope and couldn't fit his eyes over them, then he covered one eye and looked through one tube with the other. "Wow," he said. "It's reproducing as I watch. What is it, some kind of accelerated cancer culture?"

"Bingo," said the Beast. Then he turned to Jono and said, "Chamber, take all of these slides out very carefully in this sealed red bag. Then vaporize them and bury the ashes."

Jono dutifully went off to do just that.

With Jono gone, McCoy turned to the headmaster and the trooper, "It's the Legacy Virus, and it's now in an advanced state. Have you heard of it, Mike?"

"Yeah." Very few people hadn't heard of it. "That's the one that mostly hits mutants."

"Got it in one."

"Where'd that culture come from?" Trooper Brown asked.

"From that boy's spinal column," the Beast indicated the sleeping figure on the gurney beside him.

The cop squeezed his eyes shut and scrunched up his forehead, suddenly as depressed as the headmaster seemed. The boy here had to be a mutant, to have the Legacy Virus. McCoy was a mutant, and so, obviously, was Jono. That meant the rest of them probably were, too. Somehow, the knowledge did not disturb him. He had always thought that mutants were dangerous. Knowing they had the same problems and feelings as everybody else made them seem more *human*.

For his part, the Beast decided that the malaise around this place was a result of the sheer awfulness of the fate that awaited Walter. That was his first misdiagnosis in years.

McCoy would leave some painkillers with Sean, he said, but from what they knew about Statis's powers, they would help him more. "Like I told you before, the electrostatic subtext that suffuses his body," McCoy said, "should keep him coherent and without significant pain up until almost the very end. The problem with that, though, is that he'll see everything coming. I'll be checking back with you when I can."

Sean nodded blankly.

"Can I hitch a ride again, Trooper?"

McCoy and Brown were out the door and down the road well before seven in the morning. On the way, he finally got some sleep and snored thundering Beastly rales that made the windows of the car shudder. Trooper Brown stopped along the way for some coffee and secretly hoped someone on the street might spot the sleeping passenger in the state police car. Maybe someone did.

Back at the school, Walter, feigning sleep on the gurney, realized that he could count his remaining days on his fingers and, if he was really lucky, he might get to use a few of his toes.

*   *   *

The next day, Paige Guthrie tapped out her little staccato on the door of Walter's room.

"C'mon in, Paige." Walter recognized her knock by now.

She entered the room, holding a single trillium in a small plastic flowerpot in her hand.

"I'm glad you're awake," she said, making a show of trying to fight back tears but not really pulling it off. They streamed down her cheeks like a breaking river. "This is a very rare flower called a trillium."

"From the biosphere," Walter said. It seemed he had been sick as long as he had these powers. There were good days and bad days. The days for him—what few there had been—had been mostly good since he arrived here. Today was one of the bad ones. He felt it was important, though, to keep himself warm under the covers so he didn't shiver or cough too much when these depressive mutants wandered in.

"No, not from the biosphere," Paige said, "it's a New England plant." The trillium was a delicate flower with three little blue tear-shaped petals coming off a single stem as narrow as a thread. "They're rare," she said. "They mostly grow at high altitudes." She placed it on the table next to his bed.

"Really? Where'd you get it?" He tried to sound interested in the answer.

"In the woods at the base of the mountain. They're protected, you know."

"Protected?"

"Yes. It's illegal to pick them. I was careful. I got

the whole root out and took the soil it was used to," her bottom lip started to quiver. "I broke the law for you, Walter." Paige suddenly ran from the room, crying.

There was definitely something wrong here besides his Legacy Virus, Walter concluded.

At about ten that morning, the Federal Express truck rolled up to the front gate and dropped off several parcel's of clothing and other goodies. Whoever ordered it had waived a signature, so the delivery person simply left them there. No one bothered to go out to retrieve them.

CHAPTER NINE

THE BARRINGTON MILLS HOTEL

Jono blasted the alien invasion force into oblivion and almost captured their High King when his trigger finger cramped and his eyes felt tired. He saved his game, planning to rescue the President's daughter another day.

As he turned off the computer, he heard the wail of a volunteer siren. Somewhere, people were interrupting conversations, leaving in the middle of meetings, cutting short phone calls, dropping off passengers in the middle of nowhere, all to join the volunteer force whose job it was to deal with the emergency. Something was wrong in town. Which town? It was too far away to be Snow Valley.

Then he heard a siren from another direction.

Then another.

Then finally the Snow Valley sirens began along Route 9A.

Jono walked out of the computer building. He saw Emma sitting quietly in the grass near where the gazebo had once stood and where nobody had bothered so much as to lift a stick of wood to fix it. Monet swung slowly back and forth like a pendulum on the higher of the uneven bars near the edge of the woods. Paige absently picked up flat stones to skip over the fast-moving surface of the swelled Mad River. Sean sat in a porch chair, watching his inert, unringing cell phone on the chair's arm. Jubilee sat cross-legged against the wall of the biosphere looking at some book whose pages she had not turned in hours. Penance was somewhere out of sight.

After a few minutes Walter came out the side door nearest the infirmary. He wore a coverall and used an I-V rack to help him with his growing limp. He wheeled his crutch along the flagstone and Jono walked up to help him.

"Where do you need to go?" Jono asked him.

"Aren't those emergency sirens?" Walter wanted to know.

"Yeah."

"Well nobody here seems to notice. What's wrong with these people?"

Jono rattled his head as if waking from a bad dream and looked around. "Dunno," he said. "We'll deal with it after the emergency's over."

The great palaces of America were the hotels of New England. All along the interior mountains and river valleys through the nineteenth century, the merchants in the wealthy folks' destinations built great vacation hideaways. They were all of the same type: ponderous structures with white pillars, endless porches, and enormous entryways with rotundas high overhead. The suites were the size of great houses and to their institutional kitchens came many of the great chefs of the world. During weekdays in summer, tall, milk-skinned women in sun dresses and parasols would walk through the manicured lawns and gardens watching their children frolic and ride ponies in the sunshine and clean air. On weekends their husbands would travel by train from their terribly successful businesses in Boston and Hartford and New York to join the families for a few precious hours of scant involvement and rest.

Most of the palace hotels were gone now, to fires and insurance scams. There came a time when people no longer wanted to take their summers with long stretches of repose and gluttony. People wanted trips to the Caribbean and the South Pacific. Walking tours of the Old World. Time share and golf and adventure. It was easy to lose a New England palace. They were made of wood. Their kitchens vented the old fashioned way, through a single breakaway tin pipe up a flue. The fire departments were volunteer and dependent on the responsibility of the local townspeople. Only a handful or fewer of the old palaces remained.

One that remained was one of the biggest, the Barrington Mills Hotel at the base of a ski resort in southwestern Massachusetts. It looked as though it was not long for this world back in the mid-1980s, when New England real estate had hit a fifty-year peak and everyone with any assets at all was leveraged out to the next century. For the first time in living memory, people were starting to unload houses and commercial property for just a little bit less than they paid for it. Tourism and real estate were off. The very wealthy had taken to buying second homes rather than rubbing elbows with the public in hotels. The old Barrington Mills Hotel was ripe for a fall. That was when Channing Murdock, the guy who ran the ski resort, bought it for the value of its insurance policy minus the legal fees it would have cost its previous owners to make a case that the fire they planned was an accident. In short, Channing got it for a song, then he turned it into a bunkhouse.

All through the 1980s, the grand old Barrington Mills Hotel was the ten-dollar-a-night home for hundreds of itinerant skiers. Virtually all of them bought lift passes somewhere every day, and the ski areas of southwestern Massachusetts had never done better. On the big wide porch, kids strummed guitars and played boom-boxes and worked on their winter tans and came on to each other. In the old hotel suites layer upon layer of triple-decker bunk beds sat so that four six-bed rooms would meet in a common lounge with couches, a television, a pay phone and four bathrooms. The hotel's ancient venerable kitchen was the kingdom of Peter Bossert who had once reigned over the kitchen at Durgin Park. Chef Peter was a German Swiss emigré—he was still a reserve captain in the Swiss Army—enamored of thickly proteined New England fare, who ran a tight ship among the dozen or so sous-chefs of the new old Barrington Mills Hotel.

Not tight enough, as it turned out. The newest sous-chef was a young guy named Karl, who mainly took the job to meet women. The previous weekend, he had met a charming young woman on the slopes. She had agreed to have a late dinner with him that night, and his mind was on that as he mixed by hand a big bowlful of potato chunks with the contents of a two-gallon mayonnaise jar.

He didn't notice when the grease fire on the big stove caught the chef's hat he had left hanging off a cabinet. He didn't notice when the fire from the hat spread to the cabinet, then to the wall. He sniffed a bit at the smoke that wafted under his chin as he mixed. Outside, Peter Bossert played boccie with his daughter. By the time he happened to look up and notice the column of black smoke that rose from the kitchen flue, Karl's lungs were full of smoke and his face, limp in his mixing bowl, was full of potato salad.

"What can you do?" Chamber asked Walter. "Can you, like, ride a lightning bolt over there and see what the trouble is?"

"What do you mean? Fly?" Statis said. He sat in a wide chair. "I couldn't fly if I were healthy. What about that jet rig I saw you fooling with the other day?"

The two boys had run up to Banshee's office and flipped on a "Plectron," a limited-channel radio that scanned for broadcasts over the emergency bands to let volunteers know where they might be needed. The property of the local police department, the Plectron looked like a piece of primitive art among Sean's collection of high-tech gadgetry. It told them about the four-alarm fire at the Barrington Mills Hotel.

"That galvanized steel thing that burns my feet?" Jono asked. "Might as well take Sean's Humvee and fight the traffic."

"Gotta be a better way than . . . look, these guys can't

be complete zombies,'' Walter said. "They're mutants. Which of them can fly?''

"Sean. M. And Everett can do pretty much anything, but he's in Boston.''

"Let's get Sean. He's a big guy. He could carry us both.''

Chamber looked Walter in the eye and said quietly, "You're not going anywhere.'' Then he ran out the door of the building to the porch.

Walter tried to get up from his seat, plopped back, and felt his bones rattle against each other. *This is no fun*, he thought, but he had to agree with Jono.

Outside, Jono stood over the seated form of Sean Cassidy. "Come on, Sean, let's go.''

Sean began to rock forward and back, fingering his cell phone. "Never rings. Never rings,'' he said.

"It rings constantly,'' Jono contradicted. "It just isn't ringing now. And what if it did? Would you notice?''

"Be nice if it rang but it never does.''

"Sean, we've got an emergency. There's a big fire in Barrington Mills. You've got to get me there.''

"Never rings.''

Jono thought quickly. "Wait here,'' he said, then ran back into the main building and snatched the receiver of a remote phone off an end table.

"Any luck?'' Walter asked.

Jono didn't answer, but dialed the number of Sean's cellular phone instead.

He stood, listening while it rang. He got impatient and

walked outside with it. The cellular service interrupted to say that the subscriber at that number was not near the phone. Jono dialed again, standing next to Sean who smiled, watching the phone.

It rang once, twice, three times as Sean slowly reached for it and suddenly snatched it up, pushed the online button and said, "Gotcha this time."

"Sean," Jono said, "it's Chamber."

Sean looked perplexed, looked up at Jono who pointed at the receiver. Sean smiled, returning to the cell phone.

Jono projected his "voice" psionically so Sean could only hear him through the phone, despite being right next to him.

"Sean," Jono said, "there's a big fire at the hotel in Barrington Mills. The bunkhouse with hundreds of people staying there. You've got to take me there. I can take care of it if I can get there in time."

"An emergency," Sean said thoughtfully.

"Yes. Will you fly me there?"

"No thanks," and Sean clicked off.

Jono might have argued with him, or just stood over him in silent criticism, but he didn't have the time for either. Monet still swung back and forth on the uneven bars. At least she was moving.

"Hey, M!" Jono projected his voice across the big yard as he walked toward her. He made it sound as though he was standing just beneath where she swung.

Her lips moved but he couldn't hear what she said.

"Monet!" he said as he ran close enough so there

could be two sides to this conversation. "Monet, I need a ride."

"Take the Humvee."

"I've got to get to the big hotel fast, M."

"I've got exercising to do." She swung her legs list-lessly as proof.

"You'll get good exercise. I'll ride on your back and you'll fly me to Barrington Mills."

"That's just a twenty-minute drive. What kind of exercise is that?"

"If I hold on tight it's a two-minute flight."

Monet sighed. "I just wish somebody would turn off those sirens so I can exercise in peace."

"Now you're talking, lass." Jono found something to hang onto. "We're going to go find the people that're wailing those sirens and quash them."

"Really?" Monet swung idly back and forth.

"Really. You just drop me off over the hotel and I'll take care of it."

In her next forward swing she flipped off the bars. She landed in front of Jono and draped his arms over her shoulder, saying, "Hold on tight."

They were high above the trees before he could blink. It was all he could do to keep from tumbling off her. The sweep of the wind in his ears was more unnerving than the sirens.

The Barrington Mills Hotel was in chaos. There were volunteers all over the place, but the only place to draw water was the Housatonic River, a mile and a half from the fire. Even hooked up in series, all the fire hoses in the inventories of the volunteer forces of all the towns that were alerted reached barely half that distance.

One volunteer chief had the idea of hooking the hoses as far as they'd go and shooting a stream of water up at a fifty-five degree angle for the maximum possible distance. It was a valiant idea, though not likely to work, but they got busy screwing the hoses end to end, when a strange apparition appeared out of the sky to the north.

Chamber felt the heat high above the blazing hotel. As he balanced himself, sitting astride Monet's shoulders, he unwrapped the bandages around the lower part of his face, revealing a cauldron of energy far hotter than the fire below. He let the bandages hang out the back of his jacket and undid the Velcro strips that sealed his shirt over the roiling inferno of his chest.

"My stop," the artificial sound of his voice manifested in a little pocket of space alongside Monet's ear.

The fireball with limbs and a head tumbled from the flying girl's back into a flat spin toward the ground.

Jono projected currents of heat in all directions, slowing his fall, directing his spin so that he soared on the waves of the air. He made a stream of heat with a shoot of white-hot flame and rode it like a jetstream in a corkscrew pattern toward the ground. As he soared, he loosed pillars of heat at the mountains of ice surrounding the building. With each of these bolts he was rattled upward, but he did not fight it; it slowed his descent, and he had learned that flowing with the impact of his own power was the only way to keep that power from eating away at more of his flesh.

With each bolt that tumbled from the figure falling through the sky, a chunk of ice surrounding the hotel melted away. A pillar of wet steam rose to smother a piece of the fire beside it.

Around and around Chamber floated, bumping himself back upward with each exhalation of psionic heat. And each hot breath blew more of the fire out as if it were a gargantuan birthday candle.

Great draughts of steam and mist rose from the fiery hotel. Forty-six responsible citizens in surrounding towns called the Berkshire County emergency line to report a tornado touching down somewhere in the vicinity of Barrington Mills.

Jono crashed through the midpoint of the now-dying fire, the blackened hole of the roof where the kitchen flue used. Landing on the uppermost floor of the hotel, he saw charred pieces of wall and ceiling all around him. He made his way through the building itself until he found himself at the source of the flames, the kitchen where Karl Wessel had rolled over from the aluminum countertop and under a metal shelf in a puddle of water. Jono found no one else in the building. He rolled Karl on his back and felt for a pulse. He couldn't find one, but Jono's sense of touch was not the greatest in the world. He saw that Karl was breathing shallowly and pushed down hard on his chest cavity three times. From the smell of Karl's breath, Jono was almost thankful that he did not have the ability to give the man mouth-to-mouth resuscitation. After a moment Jono found a pulse.

Jono heard the crashing of feet and the chatter of voices outside the room. Quickly, he zipped up his shirt, snapped his jacket, and rolled the bandages over his face and neck to shield the energy inside. Two volunteers with axes smashed their way into the room.

Jonothon stood and said, "This man needs resuscitation," and both firemen rushed to Karl's aid. Then Jono slipped out of the kitchen.

Outside was a chaotic whirl of tromping feet and heavy equipment. Firefighters and rescue crews ran in with axes and out with heavy-breathing people. Jono walked out unnoticed. The hotel was relatively intact; only a column up the center was really destroyed. Jono suspected that with an insurance claim the owners could rebuild before next season. He hoped they did.

"Monet?" he looked around for the tall girl. Jono searched for her amidst the milling confusion of the crowd.

She was neither on the ground nor in the sky. She had left, relieved, presumably to resume her absent-minded displacement activity on the uneven bars as soon as the sirens ended.

Jonothon managed to hitch a ride close enough to home in the back of a volunteer's pickup truck. His mood could generously be described as foul.

As the truck drove toward Snow Valley, rain started to patter gently, the end result of his impromptu steam bath.

CHAPTER TEN

MAKE A WISH

C ontrary to his nature, Walter was seriously peeved. "See, the point of my being here, whether you know it or not," Walter said in a calm but clearly exasperated tone of voice, "is that it was kind of a dream of mine."

Walter had been forced to herd his teachers and fellow students into the living room the way he herded cattle back home. One by one, he had made it easier for each of them to come in here and sit down than to do whatever they were doing elsewhere. It was difficult, given Walter's infirm condition, to pull off, but he managed it.

He had first gone up to Sean and asked him to call everyone together. Sean had responded by launching into a slow, droning collection of observations on meetings and how important they were. So Walter had zapped him with enough of a jolt of static electricity to make him jump involuntarily. After being forced to jump out of his seat a few times he started to realize that it was annoying. So at Walter's suggestion, in order to avoid the exertion of continual jolting and jumping, Sean had simply gotten up and wandered in here. It hadn't even seemed to occur to Sean to resist or object or even fight back in any way. *Was this really an X-Man?* Walter wondered. He managed to do the same thing to all of them, except for Penance who followed the rest of them in out of habit.

"I was always told I was a kinda super hero. I had the mutant powers of a super hero—well, a minor super hero, but powers anyway. And my folks and this ghost back home told me all my life I had to be careful not to waste my talents, whatever they were. And here I was, nearly sixteen years old and strong and tough and ready to rock and roll—and I find out I've got this killer disease and I haven't got any time to fight Skrulls over the towers of New York or something. But I had time to come here.''

He looked around at the apathetic, wandering faces. They all stared blankly at him, except for Penance, who stood on the stone apron of the fireplace where she would do a minimum of damage. She was not tall enough for Walter to see her head reflected in the big mirror over the mantel, but there was an actual arc of darkness along the bottom of the mirror. She seemed to steal the light from her reflection.

''Here, because, besides the Legacy Virus, what I've got is a gift, see?''

With some pain the boy got up from the soft chair near the fireplace and clapped his hands together. A great white light radiated in concentric circles from Walter's palms, crackling the air and standing everyone's hair on end for a moment before it dissipated. Only Emma reached up absently to straighten her hair with a hand.

''A gift,'' he repeated, ''like all of you have got. You know how sometimes little kids with bone cancer or leukemia get to make a wish and get it granted? They get to go to Disneyland with Michael Jordan or they get to fly a plane for a few minutes while the pilot sits next to them. Well I figure this is my wish. You guys are my compensation for getting a bad hand.

"Look, the last thing I want to be around here—around anywhere—is a victim. And the last thing I need to do is talk to myself. I grew up on the prairie where there's plenty of empty space to mouth off to. But I know somewhere in there—" Walter put the flat of his hand on Sean's dense head of hair "—is a mind that's taking it all in.

"You're people of power. Great power. All of you. Now something is sucking you dry. I don't know what, but I'm convinced it's not the ghosts of some sort of dead predecessors. It's not that. I feel it in my gut. So here's what you're all going to do. Banshee, you're going to let loose a humongous ultrasonic holler just over twenty-thousand vibes a second and another infrasonic yell whose wavelength is under eighteen. That won't hurt anyone here but it's going to flush any physical foreign creatures who can hear it at all right out of here. Jubilee, I want you to flood the room with light. Blinding light. And watch for anything unusual. I know there's somebody or something here. You can find him, Jube, I bet you can. Husk," Walter turned to Paige, "have you ever morphed into something non-corporeal? Like a ghost or a mist or something?" He paused. "Paige?"

Like everyone else, she absently focused on a rough-surfaced ceramic tile in the ceiling, wondering if all the tiles were machined to have identical rough surfaces or if they were random patterns.

"All right. Well Paige, you morph into something and see if you can catch anything that manifests in the sound or the light. It's in this room. I know it is, and it's trying to make us all into zombies but it can't. Right? Monet you do the same thing. Use your speed and super-strength. And Penance, same thing. We'll try snatching at whatever it is with the non-corporeal mass of Paige and the super-corporeal mass of Penance, as well as with M's super-strength. And Emma, maybe you could snatch onto the thing using some kind of mind control. Or wing it, I guess."

He looked around. He thought they all heard him. *Let's find out.*

"Okay, sounds like a plan. We've got to move fast now . . . let's . . . go!"

Nothing. Emma looked like maybe she turned her head a little, but that was it.

"All right, maybe I didn't give you enough notice. All together now. Three. Two. One. Go!"

Nothing. Not even a rustle.

Every bone of Walter's body and every cell of his flesh ached with the encroaching Legacy Virus. And finally, with a rush of power born not of energy but of frustration, Walter raised his hands in the air, threw his head back and his midsection forward and his eyes clapped tight to shut out the pain and he expelled a wave of electrical fire and light that ionized the very molecules of the air and he hollered:

"Like . . . *this*!"

And Walter brightened the room in a uniform light that threw no shadows.

And the air rang with a deafening sound that a person could feel with every molecule.

And the heat hit the room with a tremendous blast of warmth.

And the very space seemed to shift, to offer the kind of disorientation you get sleeping through an earthquake or waking through a dream, where profound change is all around and taking you with it.

And something took shape in the air just above Walter—something almost human-looking.

And Chamber, muddied and sopping, chose that instant to walk in the door. "What's that?" he asked, pointing in the direction of Statis—

—who collapsed on the floor as the disorientation swept him away.

Chamber ran into the room. "What was that figure standing over Walter?" he demanded. "What went on here?"

Slowly turning her head in Walter's direction, Jubilee said, "Poor guy. He's always giving speeches and falling down." She took a long breath and said, "Maybe he shouldn't talk so much."

"You look terrible," Monet told the astonished Chamber. "You need a shower. You do take showers, don't you?"

"Steam baths," Jono snarled as he felt for a pulse in Walter's neck. It was slow, but steady. He had depleted his energy, sapping the reserve strength he had been using to allay the more baneful effects of his illness.

Chamber ran to the infirmary and came back with a hypo of the tincture of Vicodin that the Beast had prescribed as a painkiller if Walter needed it.

After applying it, he moved toward Sean's office. Chamber was running on the residual psychic boost he had gotten from saving lives at the old hotel less than an hour ago. Coming back to this place, though—this school that had always been a safe nesting place to him—it seemed as if a kind of depressed cloud hovered at the back of his brain. He was a little depressed to start with; conditions generally unbecoming a super hero, if the fantasy literature of his childhood was any indication. But this was something palpable he had not noticed before. He had to keep moving before it caught up with him.

Chamber ran up to Sean's office. It was locked.

It was never locked.

Since when is Sean paranoid?

He thought back at the quiet roomful of shifting eyes and blank stares he'd just left.

Everybody else is paranoid. Finally Chamber was at home. It made him feel. . . .

He wasn't sure how it made him feel, so he stopped thinking about it.

Jono broke into Sean's office with an ease that would probably depress Banshee if he ever got over whatever funk he was in. The headmaster had a visual identification program on his hard drive somewhere. It was modeled after those mug shot packages at police stations that had started to replace police sketch artists. You feed information on a face or an object into the system and it assembles a composite based on your description. But it goes one step further: it can thumb through a database and identify possible matches from a mug file. Sean got the program from some old Interpol contacts.

He started to feed in what he had seen of the figure in the white shadows that stood over Walter when Chamber walked into the room.

When Walter woke up, there was no change in the living room of the school. Everyone sat or stood in the same places in primarily the same positions they were before Walter lost his temper and his consciousness. No difference except for the tap-tap-tapping coming from the direction of Sean's office.

"What're you doing?" Walter asked Chamber, somewhat out of breath after making the walk to Sean's office.

"Finding the bad guy," Jono snorted in his hollow artificial voice. "When I came in, I saw what seemed to be a guy standing over you. You were keeling over by that time, but I gave you a shot of Hank's magic elixir." Jono tapped away at the keyboard or studied the screen with squinted eyes as he talked.

"Thanks, I guess," Walter said. He thought about what Jono said. "A guy standing over me, huh? Sure it wasn't a lady? Maybe a projection of Emma's astral form or something."

''No. This is an extradimensional demon, I think.''

Walter blinked. ''A what?''

''A demon. I've found it in the X-Men's database,'' and Chamber got up to take Walter by the arm and walk him over to the computer monitor. Walter saw a scan of an old graphic: the head of a black hooded creature with a bleach-white alien face. It had distinctive marks on both sides of its mouth, each shaped like a goat's hoof.

''What is it?'' Walter wanted to know.

Chamber said, ''According to the database, it's called D'Spayre, of all things. Cyclops once—''

A sudden din from the living room interrupted him. They both ran into the room just in time to see furniture fly into walls. Bodies clapped in repeated sickly thuds on the walls and the ground. The ground itself began to shudder.

The house sounded like it was tearing itself apart.

CHAPTER ELEVEN

SECOND DATE, THIRD BASE

"The biggest part of Everett's charm," Angelo explained, "is that he's sooooo ugly people love to be around him so they can feel superior. Real real way ugly." He pronounced the word as if it had a long U. "You gotta call him yoogly, right? Look at him."

Everett grinned.

The four of them were in a little place off Harvard Square called Mr. Bartley's Burger Cottage. It was one of those safe lunch places where the menu claimed to offer "the best hamburgers in the universe." They were certainly the best hamburgers Everett had dug into since he left Missouri, where folks knew about good burgers. The plate glass windows let in just enough of the light and the passing parade of Massachusetts Avenue. The surroundings were simple and clean polyurethaned wood and aluminum.

Angelo's unlovely but engaging ashen face and his irregular throaty voice attracted the attention of an audience larger than just Amanda, LaWanda, and the object of his tirade, Everett.

"This is not a face you want to take home to Mom," Angelo gestured at Everett's glowing movie-star looks. "It's more like a face you want to tack up on a dart board. Am I right, girls?"

LaWanda nodded and giggled a little.

"That smile is deadly," Angelo went on to a growing audience of Bartley's patrons and staff. "So deadly, in fact, that the President called up last year. You know, when that comet came through? The one nobody really saw because it was such a dud? Well the Prez had inside information, see, that this comet was gonna be a big old wangdoodle of a sucker and it was gonna thrash its tail right across the face of the Earth and whip up hailstorms and earthquakes and make the children cry and you'd have to tie down all your livestock and it was gonna cause an awful stir. So the President hired old Everett here to wring the tail off that comet by smiling it down. What? You don't believe me?"

Amanda cocked her head and creased her eyes and Angelo was almost too distracted by it to continue. But he did.

"You didn't see any hailstorms or panic in the streets, did you? See, the shuttle mission—I think it was *Atlantis*—this shuttle mission around the time of the comet with the Congressman aboard, remember that? Come on, you remember."

Angelo looked at Amanda. He looked at LaWanda. Then back at Amanda again.

"Wait, that's right," Amanda said. "They did send a Congressman up in space last year. I remember. The guys on the news said they were going to use him as ballast."

"There you go," said Angelo, "proof positive."

Everett buried his face in his hand but LaWanda took his hand and held it because she wanted to look at his face some more.

"There was no Congressman on that shuttle mission," Angelo went on. "They just said there was because the President used the Congressman to sneak

Everett here on board. And when they all got up there in space and they saw the comet coming, old Everett went out the hatch in a space suit and just smiled at that comet until it put its tail between its legs like a scared dog. The world was saved. Everett, show the ladies your Congressional Medal of Honor. Come on, show them.''

"Actually," Everett said, and couldn't say anything more.

Because Angelo said, "Modest, huh? Don't carry it around with you like I carry around my Oscar, do you? Well, that's another story. Then show these ladies the smile that scared the comet. Come on, man, smile.''

Everett clenched his teeth in a grimace. "I am smiling," he said.

The ladies giggled. The audience swelled. No one in Bartley's would get so much as a burger or a French fry until Angelo released his growing audience. This was a super-power too, of sorts.

"What about that time we were camping out in the Berkshires?'' Angelo was hot tonight. "Remember that time, Everett?''

"Which time was that, Ange?''

"That time in the tent, Ev. When you got hungry and you wanted a midnight snack in the middle of the north woods.''

"Oh that time. Sure.''

"Right. And Everett gets up and goes out at like one in the morning looking for protein. And he's walking through the dark woods and he sees this shadow on the crook of two big branches of a tree and he realizes it's got to be a squirrel. I mean, what else can it be, right?''

''Yummy,'' Everett said.

Both girls grimaced and so did most of the burger-eaters listening.

''And it would be a simple thing for Everett to snatch this big wad of protein out of the tree, see, but he realizes the squirrel or whatever it is, is sitting stock still. It's scared of him already. So he decides he's going to smile it down. He's going to smile this thing out of the tree. So he whips out his pearly whites and tries to zap this squirrel with the fear that his ugly—let me restate that—that his yoogly face engenders in this innocent furry little ball of protein.''

Angelo loved an audience. His audience enjoyed being loved.

''I mean the squirrel wasn't falling out of the tree or anything, but it was encouraging him because obviously it was scared stiff. Literally scared stiff. It wasn't moving a muscle. It wasn't twitching a hair. It was just looking back at Everett's scary smile looking back at it. So after about twenty minutes of this Everett figures he's in it for the long haul, see, and he sits down on the grass and the leaves at the foot of the tree and keeps smiling at it. He's careful. He doesn't look away for a moment. He doesn't cut that squirrel even a little break. He doesn't break that smile for an instant. Smile for the nice people, will you bro'?''

''I am smiling,'' Everett snarled.

''See? Can you look away from that smile? Can you look away from a train wreck? Fergeddabaddit. Sure as hell a squirrel can't. Not that squirrel anyway. So by now, Everett's not even thinking about the fact that he's hungry. That doesn't bother him even a little. He's not smiling down this squirrel for his hunger. He's not smiling him down for his pride. He's not doing it for the practice or the boredom or the principle. He's in it for the glory. If it takes him until the sun rises in the west he's gonna smile that squirrel down until it falls dead at his feet.

"So it's two in the morning and Everett's still sitting there smiling down the squirrel. And it's three in the morning and Everett's still sitting there smiling down the squirrel. And it's four in the morning and Everett's still sitting there smiling down the squirrel. And it's five in the morning and the sun's starting to poke its fingers over the horizon and Everett's bleary, but he's one stubborn sucker, and he's still sitting there smiling down the squirrel. And through his bleary eyes and in the first light of dawn he realizes what he's been staring at isn't a squirrel. It isn't anything like a squirrel. It isn't an animal at all. It's a knot in the bark of the tree just below where the two big branches diverge. He's been spending his smile on a big block of wood. And he looked down—"

Angelo looked over his audience and paused just long enough for them to have a moment to wonder what he was going to say next before he said it.

"—and all the bark from the trunk of the tree was lying on the ground where he had smiled it down."

The room burst into applause.

SECOND DATE, THIRD BASE

"Ugly guy," Angelo crowed, "real yoogly." Everett clapped him on the back with the hand that LaWanda wasn't squeezing.

"Can we have our burgers now?" Everett asked plaintively.

It got to be evening very quickly in Harvard Square. There was an old parking garage on John F. Kennedy Street around the corner that some enterprising developers bought and converted into a shopping mall called, aptly enough, the Garage Mall. In a science fiction bookstore in the Garage called Pandemonium, Angelo bought Amanda a book.

"I love this guy," she said, pointing at a short story collection by Orson Scott Card, so he bought her the book. Looking at the table of contents, she pointed to "Unaccompanied Sonata." "I never read this short story before. It must be new."

"No it's not," Everett looked over LaWanda's shoulder. "It's pretty old. It's a great story."

This prompted a lengthy discussion of the relative merits of Card as they walked out onto JFK Street and headed back toward Harvard Square. As Angelo and Everett went back and forth as to what, exactly, the story was about (Angelo thought politics, Everett thought music), they jagged to the left, crossing onto Brattle Street, following the girls toward the outskirts of the Square. Darkness had long since dropped over the streets of Cambridge and the four navigated by street light. The notion might have tripped into Skin or Synch's consciousness that they were wandering into a less-safe neighborhood, but these two had no practical reason to be afraid. They were actually enjoying showing off their smarts a little bit to these two college babes.

On a dark stretch of Brattle Street somewhere out past Radcliffe Yard before you could see the bright lights along Memorial Drive, Amanda wheeled around, grabbed Angelo—in the middle of a rant directed at Everett's critical acumen—by the front of his shirt and pressed her mouth to his.

Everett watched Angelo and Amanda. It went on. LaWanda watched Everett watching Angelo and Amanda. Slowly, Everett started to smile.

"You like it?" LaWanda asked Everett.

"Looks nice," Everett said.

"Try it."

He did.

They found a patch of grass on the side of a mostly darkened apartment building in which to conduct their interaction. After an hour, Everett and LaWanda lay on the grass, counting stars.

"Hey, the meeting's already started," LaWanda sat up and looked at the watch on Everett's arm that read *8:40.* "We were supposed to bring doughnuts or chips or something."

"Meeting?" Everett asked.

"Yeah, we wanted to bring you with us. It's this group we belong to."

"What, like a Tupperware club or something?"

SECOND DATE, THIRD BASE

She scrambled up to her feet, put her hands on her hips, and asked, "Do I *look* like a Tupperware party kind of girl?"

Everett smiled. "I guess not. So where are we going?"

"A meeting at Pat's place." She pointed at a three-story apartment building on Mount Auburn Drive. Everett could see that all the lights on the third floor were lit.

"Pat? Who's she?"

"He," LaWanda corrected. "Patrick Harrowhouse. He's a great guy. Smart and very articulate. He reminds me of Angelo." And she added, "And you too, of course."

"Of course."

"But I forgot to pick something up. It's pot luck."

"Hey Angelo," Everett hollered, "they want to take us to a party."

There was a rustling in the shrubbery near the edge of the big lawn. Then Angelo popped up, tucking the tail of his shirt back into his pants as he said, "Party? Where? You didn't say anything about a party."

Amanda rose languorously from behind some brush, twisting her neck from side to side.

"Well y'know," she said, "I hadn't gotten around to that part of the conversation, I guess."

"I love parties," Angelo said taking Amanda's hand and bounding out onto the lawn to join Everett and LaWanda. "Where is it? Do we have to hail a cab? Which way to the cheese dip?"

"You guys go on in and I'll catch up with you," Everett said to LaWanda. "Doughnuts all right?"

"I can't believe how sweet you are," LaWanda told Everett. She turned to Angelo and asked, "Where did you find this guy?"

Everett volunteered to go get the party favors because he supposed he was the one in the best shape. He could probably run the fastest without getting winded. And as it happened—just for having clapped his friend on the shoulder an hour earlier—he could also do anything Skin could do. To find the doughnuts he didn't need to do much. Harvard Square was simply crawling with doughnut shops. As Amanda and LaWanda took the eager Angelo off toward the small apartment building on Mount Auburn, Everett lit off in the other direction.

Everett tried out Angelo's talents. On the dark stretch of Brattle Street at the base of the fence that wrapped Radcliffe Yard, Everett concentrated. He threw both his arms up toward the pointy brass posts at the top of the fence, and both of his hands flew upward as if disconnected from their wrists. Like twin thick catgut cables flying off a pair of fishing reels, the skin rolled up from his shoulders to the top of the fence. Everett found he could shift his weight forward to his fingertips as readily as he could shift his weight from one foot to the other. Just as the skin that a moment earlier had gloved each hand reached the far side of the height of brass, the tips of Everett's fingers weighed forward like little wrecking balls and wrapped themselves around and around the posts until they held as tight as tape.

It was dark, so no one saw him standing with the elongated strands of his arms extended up and around the brass fittings of the fence top. One foot was flat on the ground and the other up on the brick facing that formed the lower part of the Radcliffe Yard barrier. He stood there and thought a moment.

Synch had borrowed the powers of dozens of other mutants and slipped in and out of the synchronicity sheaths of hundreds of people over the past few months. But he had rarely picked up a capacity that involved distorting his body to such a degree. He found it unnerving, to say the least.

Everett twitched his nose back and forth like Samantha the witch, and he loosened the skin around his nose like Skin did sometimes, and suddenly he looked like the Wicked Witch of the West. He chuckled, tested the strength of his elongated arms, and saw that it was sufficient. He pulled tight on his wrists, levered himself upward on the pivot point of the foot that pressed against the wall and catapulted himself above the fence.

As he glided, he became aware of the heavy, faraway tips of his fingers. He closed his eyes and shifted the weight of his fingertips to his arms. The extended flesh unclenched the brass fence tips. Then it snapped back up over his wrists and hands and fingertips. For a moment his whole body tingled like a foot asleep and he didn't know whether it was from his spin through the sky or his shifting flesh. The rush he felt as his sneakers clapped down on the ground in Radcliffe Yard made him look back at the way he had come and say: "Whoa!"

Then he was off across the yard through the trees and over the rooftops, flinging an arm up at a branch and yanking himself up to swing to the next tree like the king of the jungle on a grapevine. Or he'd throw a leg up at a building dressed in ivy and ride up to the roof like Spider-Man on the prowl. And maybe somebody saw him flesh-slinging through the Cambridge evening. Probably dozens of people on the quad saw him flashing through the sky overhead. People who, if they told somebody what they thought they saw, would be believed.

So what?

He spotted a Winchell's Doughnut Shop on Massachusetts Avenue at the far end of the yard and Everett took his time getting there and back, enjoying the cool night air on his face.

When Everett arrived at the building, carrying a box of a dozen-and-a-half doughnuts—assorted, skewed to chocolate—he found an agitated Angelo pacing back and forth on the sidewalk in front of the building. His friend's fingertips flew about like ten little lassos as he paced and obsessed.

"You must have a great time, man," Everett told Angelo as he sneaked up on him from behind.

Angelo did not jump or even start. He got to the end of the westbound leg of his pace, turned, and noticed

SECOND DATE, THIRD BASE

Everett standing there. "Hi," he said. And then, "What?"

"Your powers. I was trying them on," Everett said, looking at his friend to try to determine what was on Angelo's mind. "Want a doughnut?"

"Doughnut," Angelo stared for a moment at the box of doughnuts that Everett now held open for him. Angelo looked at the eighteen little clumps of carbohydrates as though they were alien artifacts from the planet Clueless.

"Are you all right, Ange?"

"Yeah. No. I don't know."

"Take one."

"It's for them, right?"

"Well I bought them. They're for whoever I say. Take one."

Angelo took a big chocolate bear claw. He took a bite and, to Everett's disbelief, put it back in the box. Angelo *never* turned down doughnuts. He certainly didn't turn down already-chewed doughnuts.

"Angelo, what's the matter?"

Angelo's eyes shifted, looking at nothing in particular.

"Go look," he said.

"What do you mean?"

Hands wringing. Fingers flapping. Eyes shifting. He repeated, "Go look."

"Be a person!" Patrick Harrowhouse exhorted the room.

Nods of assent. Positive murmurs.

"Not a freak!" he added.

"Not a freak," somebody nodded and repeated.

Harrowhouse began again: "Be a . . ."

"Person" a few of them said.

From Harrowhouse: "Not a . . ."

"Freak," more people finished his chant.

Harrowhouse led them in the refrain: "Be a person! Not a freak!"

And they joined him: "Be a person! Not a freak!"

"Be a person! Not a freak!"

"Be a person! Not a freak!"

After a minute, Harrowhouse held up his hands, and his people eventually quieted down.

Amanda and LaWanda sat near the back of the room and toward the middle where an aisle separated rows of chairs. They saved seats for Everett, who had gone to get doughnuts, and Angelo, who had excused himself for a moment. Thirty-odd people crowded into the small residents' lounge.

There was plenty to munch on; LaWanda needn't have worried. A long table along the back of the room held three big coffee urns, cookies, cakes, lemonade, a rack of individual cans of soda, and loads of doughnuts from three different doughnut places.

Patrick Harrowhouse was a young man—a little younger than Emma, a lot younger than Sean—whose future was getting brighter by the day. There were at least a hundred people from as far north as Ipswitch and as far south as Scituate who dropped in on these meetings at least once in awhile. He'd been written up in the *Globe* twice and he had been interviewed on Channel 5 and by half-a-dozen local radio news operations. He had a short article picked up by the *Hartford Courant* last month and the *Los Angeles Times* had expressed interest until the editor realized the essay had already been published elsewhere around the country. The *L.A. Times* is a national newspaper, the editor had insisted wishfully and against all evidence, so maybe Pat should get in touch when he had something new to submit. He would. Meanwhile, as Pat would announce to these good people tonight, national figures in the Movement had taken notice of him and as of today they were a part of the international organization.

Not at all bad for a Boston College psych department dropout.

Harrowhouse had been a turn-on to Amanda and LaWanda from the moment they had heard him speak. In fact, he was the reason they were friends. They had been walking through the student lounge in their dorm and there he was on the eleven o'clock news. Someone went to change the channel and LaWanda said no, please leave it, this is interesting. Amanda agreed and it took until the end of the news feature on him before their classmates could switch to an old episode of *Murphy Brown*. The pair saw each other again at the following Monday's meeting here at the little apartment building on Mount Auburn Street and they had been inseparable ever since. Now these neat guys they had met were best friends too. It was fate, they were sure.

"Something very exciting is happening tonight," Patrick Harrowhouse was saying just as Everett walked in with his almost-full box of doughnuts. "Tonight, we're no longer just a loose collection of friends floating alone. We are *not* alone."

"Hi," Everett smiled at LaWanda. "What's with Angelo?"

"Went to the boys' room," she squeezed his hand and kissed him on the cheek. "Shh," she said as she thanked him for the doughnuts and put them on the table behind their seats.

"He's out on the—" Everett began, but Amanda leaned in to shush him—smiling but firm—and La-Wanda squeezed his hand.

"Our Movement, the very system of beliefs that makes us who we are," Harrowhouse continued, demanding eye contact by his intensity and mesmerizing his people with his voice, "unites us with our brothers and sisters across the country. It's not just desirable, it's necessary."

He grabbed a cord that dangled from a wide rolled-up bolt of cloth that hung across the low ceiling behind him.

"As we feel better about ourselves, we become more potent in the pursuit of our lives and our beliefs. So without further elaboration or ceremony, let us all join hands and look to the future as, under my authority as the first grand marshall of the Metropolitan Boston and Cape Cod region, I declare this the first official meeting of the Boston chapter of the Friends of Humanity."

"Excuse me?" Everett asked. "Repeat?"

As if in answer, Harrowhouse yanked on the cord he

held and a slip-knot released the bolt of cloth. It unrolled to reveal the big, cheerfully colored international logo spelling out in big block letters: FRIENDS OF HUMANITY. A matching blue border decorated the edge like patriotic bunting.

"We're part of a national organization now," La-Wanda gushed. "Isn't it wonderful? He says there's going to be a rally in the Square tomorrow. The first one here ever."

Friends of Humanity: the small but visibly growing anti-mutant hate group whose political power had grown to an astonishing degree in a short time. The head of the organization, Graydon Creed, was a legitimate Presidential candidate. They had the ears of senators and governors, CEOs and professors. At their best, they asserted that *homo superior* were a threat to the world's future. At worst, they were the harbingers of a worldwide holocaust and race war.

And here these normal-seeming people—LaWanda and Amanda, for pity's sakes—involved themselves because they thought this was a fun time and a neat way to make new friends.

"So let us say together," Harrowhouse smiled, closing his eyes as if floating blissfully on a cloud, "Earth for humanity!"

"Earth for humanity!" they all repeated except for Everett.

"We're humans too," Everett whispered loudly enough that LaWanda could hear.

"Of course we are," she said, not getting it.

"Be a person!" Harrowhouse exhorted again, "Not a freak!"

"Be a person!" they all repeated in rhythm, "Not a freak!"

"Be a person! Not a freak!"

Everett watched LaWanda repeating the words. Believing them. Wearing a look of profane rapture on her face. He took his hand out of hers and wiped it on his shirt.

"Be a person! Not a freak!"

He backed out the door and saw his reflection in the one-way glass pane as he closed it. He did not recognize himself.

"Be a person! Not a freak!"

LaWanda and Amanda didn't even notice his departure.

"Be a person! Not a freak!"

It seemed to grow louder from behind the closed door. He covered his ears and rushed out to the street where he found his best friend, still pacing. The ashen form of Angelo strode with wringing hands and spinning fingertips in and out of the beam of a lonely streetlight.

After a moment of watching this, and listening for the sound of the chanting which, finally, he did not hear any more except in haunting memory, Everett walked up behind Angelo.

"Want to go?" Angelo asked Everett.

"Bad party," Everett said.

"Yeah. Real bad. They're having a rally tomorrow. Could get hairy."

SECOND DATE, THIRD BASE

"Yeah?"

"Yeah," Angelo said. "Want to go?"

"Where? The motel? The rally?"

"No. I mean home."

Everett thought for a moment. "Hell no."

"Okay," Angelo shrugged. "Good call."

CHAPTER TWELVE

A TOUCH OF BRIMSTONE

Emma was lost in her mind. She had spent a lot of
time there over the years and was rather surprised
and a little bit delighted now to find that she did
not know her way around it as well as she thought. Not
long ago, she had become so lost within herself that the
world had thought her dead. When she came out of that
coma, she learned to her horror that her students the
Hellions had all been killed.

Prior to that, a fellow mutant named Mastermind—a
master illusionist—had created images in her mind so
powerful, it sent her into another coma. She dragged her
way out of that herself, and got to know herself very
well in the process.

Or so she thought.

She poked around her mind now, trying to figure out
which version of her self-image was the real one.

Chamber and Statis found Emma sitting in the biosphere, high atop one of the structure's high slats, draped
over one of the crosspieces that formed a hexagon. It
looked almost comfortable. She seemed asleep but her
eyes were wide open.

The two of them had run out of the house when the
walls shook and furniture rolled along the floors. They
could not induce anyone other than Emma to leave—
and Emma did not leave due to their urging. She simply
unfolded herself from a fetal position on the floor, stood
up, and wandered out the door while Jono and Statis
were arguing with Sean.

"It's D'Spayre!" Jono yelled at the headmaster. "We figured it out with your bad guy database. He can do stuff like this!"

"I really should upgrade the mother board to a P-7 chip," Sean mused as the walls shook. "Then it would have an easier interface with Charles's computer."

The two boys gave up on the headmaster and tried the headmistress.

Staring at her now on top of the biosphere, Jono asked, "Do you think we should bother her?"

"Don't think so," Walter said. "I ever tell you about my older brother Ian the sleepwalker?"

When she first brought the Hellions together, back when Xavier's School for Gifted Youngsters was called the Massachusetts Academy and Emma Frost was its sole owner and headmistress, she had an agenda. She saw her students, not as people, but as part of that agenda.

It wasn't until they all died that she realized that somewhere in there she had grown to love them as if they were her own children.

She had resolved to be a better person when she finally began to reassemble the shards of her composure after the Hellions were slaughtered. And she had become a better person, she decided, but only in the sense that a bad cold is better than pneumonia.

There was not that much difference, she now realized, between the White Queen who in those days presided over disaster, and the one who now trafficked with the spirits of her dead students. The agenda had simply changed a bit, from—

From what? Emma thought. *What was that all about?*

"The Hellfire Club," Jetstream said.

Emma looked up in surprise to see the young Hellion sitting with her on another slat of the geodesic structure.

"That was what you were talking about," Jetstream said. "The Hellfire Club. On the outside it was an exclusive club for the wealthiest people in the world. On the inside were rich mutants who wanted to rule the world."

"People like me," the White Queen said.

"That's right," said Jetstream.

"And when the world thought we sat around playing whist and held audiences for aspiring young politicians, what we really did was scour the world for talented young mutants to put in positions of potential power and authority. We would train them just enough to make them vaguely aware of their powers, and we would effectively brainwash them in favor of the long-term goal of gathering, as the mutant population mushroomed, a worldwide network of powerful but naïve mutants who answered only to us."

"People like me," Jetstream said.

Suddenly, Emma no longer sat in a strange structure on an isolated stretch of acreage in western Massachusetts. She stood in the walnut-paneled drawing room on the fourth floor of the Hellfire Club's Fifth Avenue headquarters. A fire crackled in the hearth. Out the window, she could see a Congressman's car and driver waiting for him. Above she could see the clouds gathering for a rainstorm.

Jetstream, poor lost Jetstream, still stood silently next to her. "Send those two in," she commanded. "Those stiff-necked ones with the fire in their bellies."

"Didn't we come out here for a reason?" Walter asked Jono from below Emma's perch in the biosphere.

"I'm sure we did," Jono replied.

"Well?"

"Well what?"

"What was it?" Statis asked.

Jono hesitated. "Are you feeling depressed?"

"I'm dying. I'm always feeling depressed." Then Statis thought for a moment and asked Jono, "Are you?"

"I've got half a face and no real voice and can barely even be thought of as a person any more," Jono said, "but I think I'm feeling a wee bit more depressed than usual, yeah."

"This D'Spayre guy," Statis said, "he makes people depressed and feeds off the energy they throw off with their depression, right?"

"That's what the file said. So you think we're feeding this cannibal?"

"Yeah."

"Depressing," Jono said. Then he looked up and noticed that Emma had started talking to herself rather animatedly.

Then both boys realized they no longer stood in the

biosphere, but in a lavishly decorated reception area that looked like it hadn't changed since it was built around the Revolutionary War. The sounds of Manhattan traffic could be heard from outside, and Jono noticed Central Park across the street through the huge picture window.

The huge oak double doors opened and a tall dark young man stood before them wearing the distinctive purple-and-black uniform of the Hellions. "She will see you now," he said. "Follow me."

Statis and Jono exchanged glances. They both recognized the boy as Jetstream. Shrugging, they followed the young dead mutant into the large dim room containing a softly crackling fireplace, a score of painted portraits of long-dead rich mutants, all well above eye-level. The most beautiful woman either boy had ever seen sipped an amber liquid in a half-filled brandy snifter.

They had to take a few steps toward her before realizing that the woman was Emma Frost. Statis was embarrassed by this realization. Chamber was used to it.

Jono wanted to say, *What's going on here?* Instead he asked, "Has the committee reviewed our applications yet?"

"Yes," Emma said, putting down the glass. The room was full of empty chairs and couches but Emma did not invite either boy to sit down.

Walter said, "We're eager to join your organization, Ms. Frost." He no more intended to say it than Jono had, but he couldn't help himself.

"The other committee members and I are aware of that," she said.

Silence reigned for what seemed to be a few minutes. Jetstream stood at the open door staring out into space. The boys wanted to ask how they got here, what Emma was doing here, what this application and committee they spoke of were. Instead, they stood there, unable to speak.

"Would you like to hear what it will mean to be a member of this organization, gentlemen?" she finally asked.

No, they both meant to say but said, "Yes, ma'am."

She rose imperiously and paced the room as she spoke:

"You will renounce any country or potentate or religion or family to which you have ever borne allegiance. You will renounce any personal rights or aspirations that do not also include the community of mutantkind at large. You will submit to a rigorous daily schedule of training and study that will last through the remainder of your childhood and well into your adulthood—should you live to adulthood. You will, during this period of training, be on call to participate in the dispatching of any and all threats either to our mutant community or to any part of the planet the committee or your immediate supervisors deem valuable, or any institution of the planet that we care to preserve in order to harvest or confiscate later when we execute the final political phase of our long-term plan. During this time you will routinely be exposed to dangers and risk of life and whatever measure of liberty that may remain to you. Many of your predecessors have suffered loss of life, or

health, or their very identities in pursuit of the goals we
have set during these past centuries.''

Throughout, both boys had numerous questions. Yet
they remained silent.

''Do you both willingly submit to these conditions?''
Emma asked.

Jono meant to say, *You just think you're all that and
a bag of chips, don't you, lady?*

Walter meant to say, *When pigs sprout wings!*

Instead, both enthusiastically said, ''Yes, ma'am,''
and followed Jetstream back out into the reception area.

Jono was growing what might have been a knot in
the belly, except that he had no real belly to speak of.
It grew anyway.

Suddenly, Walter spun around to smile at Jono and
made a gesture with one hand. A thin shock of static
electricity leapt from Walter's fingertips to where Jono's
belly used to be and the quick shock blew open Jono's
psionic voice.

''What the bloody hell's going on here?''

Emma stopped and looked at him. Statis grinned. Jetstream faded away into nothingness.

Again, even louder, Jono's artificial voice shattered
the illusion of the Hellfire Club with the bone-shattering
demand:

''What the bloody hell's going on here?''

With that, they found themselves back in the biosphere. It was pitch dark out. The windows and doors
of the main building flapped open in the wind, unat-
tended. Emma sat on the ground, her expression dreamy,

leaning against the inward-slanting exterior wall of the biosphere. Walter, thin and weak with veins protruding from his arms to make streaks in his tattoos, fell to the ground, exhausted but conscious.

Before Jono, a mist swirled and collected and began to form a horrible image.

A voice, whispery at first but strengthening, sounded as the mist took form. "Oh how delicious. A reaction, and an angry one, from both of you. It has been days since I injected you into the Frost creature's illusory consciousness, and finally you give me something to feed on."

Then, before Jono stood what could only be called a demon: black-and-white skin covered in rippling black.

D'Spayre.

Jonothon fell on the ground beside Walter.

CHAPTER THIRTEEN

DEMONSTRATION IN THE SQUARE

Perhaps Synch's most useful power was his uncanny ability to find a parking space under the most adverse of circumstances. Whenever Sean took the whole group somewhere, he let Everett navigate. Here in Harvard Square—possibly the most difficult neighborhood to park in north of Midtown Manhattan—he slid the little Jeep Wrangler into a space between a deli and the big triangular *Harvard Lampoon* building.

"Good old Synch, the Zen motorist." Angelo clapped his friend on the back trying to reclaim the good mood of yesterday afternoon.

Everett smiled unconvincingly, and joked, "Yes, truly I am one with the city." But his heart wasn't in it.

The pair of them walked into the deli, called Elsie's Luncheonette and found Amanda and LaWanda just as the latter ordered a Saul Bellow sandwich: pastrami and chopped liver on rye without the top slice of bread and a kosher dill pickle on the side.

"We half-thought you guys weren't going to show up," Amanda said, "after the way you just disappeared last night."

"Almost didn't," Angelo said before Everett jabbed him in the ribs.

"Did we do something wrong?" Amanda asked.

"How about your John Kenneth Galbraith for me with a Mango Madness Snapple?" Everett asked the counter woman, ignoring the question. "What about you, Ange?"

"You got something like a ham and cheese?" Angelo asked.

The woman replied, "Sounds like the Martin Luther King cheeseburger. Comes with two strips of Georgia bacon, tomato, lettuce, and mayo with peaches and cream on the side."

"Good deal," Angelo said. "Same thing they call the 'Ray Charles' sandwich back home."

"Why am I not surprised?" the counter woman asked. Angelo's right eyebrow rose—about three inches, actually—in mild offense.

"You're avoiding the question," Amanda said with a touch of sternness.

"So what's with this guy Harrowhouse?" Everett asked.

LaWanda shrugged. "We thought you'd find him interesting. Didn't you?"

"Oh yeah, he was *very* interesting," Angelo said. "Sort of like a bird thinks a python is interesting. Can't look away from him."

"Y'know, everything's not about politics, you guys," Amanda said. "Pat Harrowhouse is a charismatic, articulate guy with a message. I mean, people come to the city and they don't know anybody. They'd rather not hang out at bars and maybe can't meet anyone on the Freedom Trail—surprise, surprise. So they go to see Pat Harrowhouse and maybe meet some nice people and eat doughnuts and enjoy the show."

Somewhere in there, Everett and Angelo got their sandwiches. Synch was the only one eating his. *I should've ordered something with some meat on it*, he thought.

After swallowing his food, he said, "You're aware the Friends of Humanity is a hate group, right?"

"Well yeah, technically, I suppose." LaWanda gestured grandly. "I mean we're supposed to be against mutants taking over the world. Well, duh!"

"Duh? That's a pretty flexible term," Everett said. "Would that be 'duh' meaning 'you're not telling me anything I don't know and of course we hate mutants;' or 'duh' meaning 'you're telling me something that may or may not be true, but it doesn't matter either way;' or maybe something else altogether?"

LaWanda and Amanda looked at each other, trying to figure out the shades of logic in Everett's argument, until Amanda said, "Is this a multiple-choice test? All of the above."

"So you hate all mutants," Everett suggested, "but it's not that belly-hate like you reserve for, say, the guy that forgets to flush the toilet or the professor who gives you a C because he can't place your face to your name and figures you probably didn't show up for many classes."

"What?" LaWanda said.

"Well, sure," Amanda said. "Yeah, I guess I'd feel safer if I knew there were no blood-drinking, baby-stealing mutants around to replace humanity in a few hundred years. I'd like to think my grandchildren aren't going to get killed off in a race war. Who wouldn't? Wouldn't you?"

Everett had nothing to say to that.

"What's the deal, you guys?" LaWanda asked. "You got some stake in mutants? You got a mutant landlord or a mutant once catch your grandmother falling off a train or something? Why is this bothering you?"

"Did we say it's bothering us?" Everett asked as he picked up LaWanda's thick half-sandwich with a palm under the floppy paper plate on which it rested. "Something bothering you, Angelo?"

"Well—"

"What gives you the impression that something's bothering us?" Everett interrupted as he balanced the sandwich on the tips of his fingers.

"What are you doing with my lunch?" LaWanda asked. She was starting to sound indignant.

"You ever hear of something called the Ku Klux Klan?" Everett drew away each of his fingers one at a time until the sandwich on the paper plate balanced on just the tip of his forefinger.

LaWanda rolled her eyes. "You're comparing the Friends of Humanity to the Ku Klux Klan? Very nice. Do you juggle, too? What other tricks can you do?"

The sandwich started to turn slowly on the tip of Everett's finger.

LaWanda continued: "We don't wear masks and we don't go after any innocent people. Just creatures who aren't even human. What's wrong with that?"

The plate rose in the air, turning.

"What are you doing with my lunch?"

The sandwich rose over the plate, turning in the opposite direction.

"*I'm* human," Everett said.

Chunks of sandwich components flew in all directions. They spun in little curlicues around and through the blades of the ceiling fan. Little globules of mayonnaise whirled around, caromed off the walls in figure-eights around LaWanda and Amanda's faces.

Everett stood quietly now in the center of the room, eyes closed, concentrating. He had a bead on every molecule of every object in the room. He cupped his hands in front of himself, clapped them together—

—and every object flying around the room stopped. Changed course. Rode a beeline in the direction of Everett's clapped hands. One layer of sandwich after another assembled like soldiers above the little paper plate that still hovered, rotating slowly above Everett's line of sight.

Then all the disparate elements of what used to be half a Saul Bellow sandwich *thwock*ed together. Every crumb and particle found its spot relative to every other crumb and particle like a deck of cards rising suddenly from a game of fifty-two-pickup. Suddenly, it was once again a half of a Saul Bellow sandwich, complete with a bite precisely arranged in LaWanda's incisor pattern extracted from one side. It then gently lowered itself to the paper plate which, in turn, gently lowered itself into Everett's open left hand.

"That was a breakthrough, man," Angelo told Everett. "Sean always said you'd be able to do stuff like that—get synchronicity with inanimate objects.''

"Only when I'm really angry, I guess," Everett whispered, eyes closed and serene as a monk.

LaWanda stood with her mouth hanging open.

"That was like an illusion, right?" Amanda said hesitantly. "Like a hologram or something?"

Everett flicked the middle finger of his right hand over his thumb as though he were shooting marbles—

—and a tiny sesame seed shot out of a crust of the half-slice of rye bread, like a tiny bullet into the tip of Amanda's tongue.

"Eep!" she said, bit down and swallowed it.

"Can't taste an illusion, babe."

The woman behind the counter—who, as it happened, had been serving sandwiches for thirty years and was not surprised by much of anything—said to Everett, "Thanks for cleaning up after yourself. That's a boy from a good family." Then she continued wiping down the counter.

LaWanda finally forced out the words: "What . . . are . . . you?"

"He's a *mutie*!" Amanda hollered and grabbed her friend by the arm and bolted for the door.

Skin spun and reached for the door from across the room. His arm unravelled faster than Amanda could run and certainly faster than she could drag LaWanda along. He tapped them both on the shoulder from across the room.

"What?" LaWanda said as she and her friend stopped short. "You too? You're one too?"

"I was just wondering," Angelo said, reeling in his arm and not moving toward them, "what time did you say that rally in the Square was?"

"Noon," LaWanda said automatically. Then, realizing what a mistake it was to answer, she allowed Amanda to pull her out the door.

Perhaps a thousand people milled around Harvard Square this weekday noon. Pat Harrowhouse held a megaphone and stood on a milk crate in the center of human traffic, drawing listeners in with his amplified voice. Over one hundred people—two dozen of them from last night's meeting—stopped to listen to his invective.

"Today," he said, "we are a small band of brothers and sisters."

Stirring, positive sounds from the crowd.

"Tomorrow," he continued, "we are a movement."

Applause and scattered cheering.

"And in this generation," he went on, "we will prevail."

The crowd cheered. And over their hollering—as if to tell them to quiet down because what he had to say was more important than their positive response to it— he said: "Because we cannot afford to fail.

"Would you give away your wallet to a person who simply asked you on the street to give it to him?"

The crowd murmured.

"Of course not. Would you sell your birthright for a bowl of soup? Or your freedom for a vague possibility of peace or a job or even some measure of financial security?''

''No,'' the faithful among his listeners called out.

''Would you surrender your home to an intruder without a fight?''

''No!'' many of the crowd hollered as the newcomers began to get the idea.

''Would you surrender your children . . .''

''No way!'' an enthusiastic supporter roared in a voice louder than Harrowhouse's.

''No you wouldn't, would you? And would you surrender your children's future to a race who have terrorized innocents for years? Who tell us that they are the face of our future?''

''No!'' a hundred or more people in the courtyard of Holyoke Center in Harvard Square said as one.

The press always arrived late. Harrowhouse had been careful to start on time so that he could work this group up before they arrived. And they had better arrive—or else it didn't count. If the rally didn't make the six o'clock news, there was no point to the rally.

''No!'' his crowd roared again, even louder.

''So what do we say when some politicians present us with ballot measures allowing special rights for mutants?''

''No!''

''And what do we say when some Congressman wants to allocate public money for doctors to study some phony-baloney virus that only infects mutants?''

''No!''

"Or when the drug-swilling, gene-altering parents of a mutant kid in school with your kid, say their monstrosity is a 'special needs' student and your community has to fork over extra tax dollars to educate the Son of Frankenstein properly so he'll grow up to be a well-adjusted little abomination?"

"No!"

"And when your daughter's prom date turns out to have three lungs or two hearts or an ability to snoop on your thoughts; or when the person your child introduces as the one he or she wants to marry suddenly teleports to the store and back for a carton of milk, or shoots concussion fields from its hands, what do we say then?"

"No!"

"No!"

"No!"

A local news van rolled up Massachusetts Avenue, just as the crowd moved inexorably toward a fever pitch. Soon the other television and radio folks would arrive along with the *Globe* and the community papers. Today was the day Patrick Harrowhouse became a local hero.

And tomorrow . . . ?

Harrowhouse was playing the crowd like Nero played his violin. When you can't draw a crowd, the rule goes, you find a crowd and hold them just long enough for the press to see and the word to spread. Then the witnesses wove among them with their notebooks and their microphones and their little shoulder-held cameras to record and spread what Harrowhouse had to say.

"Humanity has always been better at enduring adver-

sity than at avoiding it. That's why we're here today.
We are here to assert that this adversity must be the
exception. If we do not avoid this adversity—this encroaching mutant race—then we will not endure them.
They will not suffer our endurance. They will replace
us."

Murmurs.

"Because replace us is what they have come here to
do."

It was still Harvard Square, but gradually these folks—
enough of them to change the nature of the air itself—
began to take on the look of a mob of pitchfork-toting
peasants.

"So here will we stand. And this ground will we hold.
And we declare from this spot and this moment that they
will not replace us. They will not supplant us. They will
never tear us from our ancient roots."

The crowd went wild.

"Are you all right up here, man?" Angelo asked.

"Yeah, this is cool as a moose," Everett said.

"What as a who?"

"Something Sean says," said Everett with a shrug,
"cool as a moose."

"Sean. Figures," Angelo said. "Man's been lost in
the Eighties since the Seventies. Come on, man. Do your
synchronicity thing."

They sat on the peak of the Harvard Coop building,
the highest point overlooking the Square. They could see
the lunch crowd milling below, and a clot of people

huddled around a guy with a megaphone standing on a milk crate. The rally seemed so little from here, so insignificant even against the backdrop of this little square in this little town. But the reporters gathering around it threatened to make it something bigger.

Unless Skin and Synch stole Pat Harrowhouse's thunder.

For luck and for power, Synch mussed the top of Skin's head—hard enough so Angelo's scalp rode his skull like a wave. But now Everett was in synch.

"Let's go," Everett said, and the pair of them dove off the rooftop toward the crowd below.

"Look! Up in the sky!" somebody said.

Everett shot out a skein of flesh. About a third of the way down toward the ground he flung an arm at the crosspiece of a streetlight. His hand and wrist lassoed the pole and he swung over the crowd in a gentle arc.

Angelo had more practice. As Everett was swinging gracefully over the marvelling crowd, Angelo power-dove into their faces. He plunged headlong at the crowd. A thousand people caught their breaths, as four limbs propelled in four directions: at a brass fence around Harvard Yard on the far side of the street; at a big aluminum sign for a restaurant, the Wursthaus, on the corner where Massachusetts Avenue doglegs at a right angle to itself; at the pole connected to the underground staircase that indicated a "T" station; and at the neck of the little gargoyle hanging under a dormitory window just inside the Yard.

No one said a word.

DEMONSTRATION IN THE SQUARE

As Angelo hung above the intersection that formed Harvard Square, Everett touched down and reeled himself together a few feet in front of an awestruck Pat Harrowhouse.

Then Angelo reached down to the ground with the leg that he unravelled from the restaurant sign. With the skin of his foot on the spot that the lunch crowd cleared for him, he began to whip his remaining limbs off the gargoyle, the pole, and the fence top. He coiled himself up and snapped his skin back in place, or as close to in place as he ever could get it.

Everett started talking. "Pat, we haven't formally met but I was at your meeting last night. Sorry I couldn't stay."

As Everett extended an open hand to the man standing on the concrete pillar, Harrowhouse recoiled and stepped back with the stage-whispered word, "Freak!"

"People call me 'Synch,' actually. As in 'synchronicity.' Get it?"

All of Boston watched through the reporters' camera lenses as a horrified Harrowhouse stepped clumsily off the back of his milk crate. Realizing his danger, he leaned forward to compensate a moment too late. He tumbled right into the arms that Everett extended reflexively to stop Harrowhouse's tumble.

The crowd simultaneously stepped back as if with a hive mind as both dropped flat on the sidewalk. They each scrambled to their feet. As Everett got out from underneath the speaker, the younger man felt something he had hardly expected to feel.

He felt mutant power.

With a moment's concentration, he could duplicate that person's special abilities, whatever they were. The person he'd touched was the racist, hate-mongering mutant-baiter, Patrick Harrowhouse.

When he realized just what that power was, Everett wondered if Harrowhouse even knew he had it. He also knew what he had to do.

"Excuse me," Everett snatched back his composure as he stood facing the crowd and—not so nominally— the cameras, "but I wonder if I could have a word with you folks for a moment."

Angelo wasn't sure what was going on, but he knew that something about Everett was different. Smoother. Clearer.

"My name's Everett and I'm a mutant," he said, smiling his smile. "We're a little different, that's true, and maybe that makes us a threat. But if you feel threatened, it's not we who threaten you. Rather it is you who threaten yourselves. And who is it you are threatened by? By my friend Angelo here whose skin stretches like silly putty?"

Angelo saw Amanda and LaWanda across the street in front of the entrance to the Harvard Coop. They walked over to where Everett spoke. Somehow, he wasn't concerned about them.

"Are you threatened by me?" Everett wanted to know. "I can tune into the wavelength of just about anybody, especially other mutants, and assume their abilities for a short time. That's how I made my entrance a moment ago, using Angelo's powers. Pretty good show, huh?''

It was something about his voice—that is, Harrowhouse's voice. A certain reverberating timbre. You wanted to listen to whatever he had to say.

''Maybe you're threatened by the kid down the block that can open a can of tuna fish with his fingernail. Or the girl who sits in your class who can tie a shoelace by thinking about it. That would get you a little disoriented, wouldn't it? But does it threaten you? I can't see why.''

Harrowhouse stood on the sidewalk without the vaguest notion of what to do. This hairless little black mutant had stolen both his audience and his thunder. Harrowhouse was no longer in control, and he didn't like it.

''Do you know that the genetic variation among mutants like Angelo and me and the scary little kid down the street who can juggle without his hands, is greater than the average variation between *homo sapiens* and mutant DNA? Let me explain that.''

He went on, and the crowd were enraptured. No one shopped or ate, no one went to class. People missed appointments to swim in the wash of oratory in which this terribly charismatic young man was bathing anyone who would listen.

''From a biological standpoint, mutants as a group are more like your garden variety human being like most of you are, than mutants individually are like one another. That's a remarkable statistic and it's absolutely true. It's the first thing people like Hank McCoy or Charles Xavier or someone doing a job like they do tells us when we're first identified. It's like being in third grade and taking an IQ test and finding out you're a gifted kid. Suddenly everybody's making a fuss over you. But it's the people around you who change when they find out what you are. Who you are hasn't changed.''

He spoke like that for about twenty minutes, until he had no more to say. He spoke of races and immigrants and the founding of the American nation. He spoke about the race of humanity—whether some medical classification called them *homo sapiens* or *homo superior*—and how they have always been a race of explorers. Humans have quarrelled and warred and worshipped false gods and pursued superstition and erred in the name of truth, but the thing humans have always done best is dare. They have crossed oceans and ventured into space; made treaties with their enemies and welcomed strangers to their tables. And they have always asked how we can grow from the next challenge.

Everett said all that. And he knew, and everyone standing in the Square knew—including the erstwhile Grand Marshall of the regional chapter of the Friends of Humanity—even if only for a moment, that what he said made sense.

Everett knew that Patrick Harrowhouse was a mutant, whether Harrowhouse himself knew it or not. He would always be able to enchant a crowd with the special energy of his words. But he would never again use it to turn masses of men and women against mutants and their institutions. By touching Harrowhouse, and by enveloping himself in synchronicity with this gifted demagogue, Everett had taken Harrowhouse's own power and used it to change even his mind.

Everett finished, and stepped down into the silent crowd. He asked Angelo, "Where did we park?"

"What?"

"The Jeep," Everett said. "Where did we leave Sean's old Wrangler?"

"Oh," Angelo said, coming out of his trance as few of the crowd around him had yet done. "Near the *Lampoon* building a few blocks that way. Want to walk over there?"

Everett looked out at the friendly but progressively denser crowd he had attracted here in Harvard Square. "I don't think we can," he said. "Let me try something."

Everett lightly closed his eyes and reached out an arm in the direction of the *Harvard Lampoon* building.

"What are you doing?" Angelo asked. "Pulling a Yoda?"

"A Yoda?"

"Yeah. Trying to lift the starship out of the swamp using the Force."

"Something like that," Everett said through closed eyes.

"Is it at all possible that you could drop it?" Angelo asked nervously.

Everett opened his eyes. "I guess it is," he said, and they stood there looking around; the crowd showed no interest in getting out of anybody's way. "Let me try something else."

Everett reassumed his pose. A minute later, a radial tire floated through the sky and descended into the Square. Then another tire. Then a steering column. Then a side of steel chassis. Then a steady stream of greasy car parts that circled as they flew over the Yard and into the Square to land in a pile on the sidewalk in front of Holyoke Center. The crowd gradually widened to make way for more and more car parts until there sat an eight-feet-wide, four-feet-high jumble of automobile components.

"I've found," Everett said to his friend as disparate chunks of car began to rotate together in the air as if they were so many parts of a deli sandwich, "that American parts fit back together more easily."

"Like you've got experience in this area," Angelo said with a snort.

The car assembled itself under Synch's tutelage. When it was again a battered but whole Jeep Wrangler, Everett and Angelo climbed into it. Slowly they edged their way through the dispersing mass of humanity.

Within minutes, they rolled onto the Mass Pike. They would be home in two hours.

CHAPTER FOURTEEN

SPIDER WEB

The last thing Chamber remembered was D'Spayre standing over him triumphantly. Now he found himself standing in, of all things, a human mouth. A very large human mouth. It was sticky here.

Jono slogged through the salivary flow on a giant tongue in a mouth just open enough to shed some light on the dangling uvula down back. It was not a lot of fun.

This is my nightmare, Jono thought.

"You think she can read our thoughts in here?" Statis asked Chamber.

Chamber whirled to find Walter Nowland standing behind him. He squinted his eyes, and would have mouthed the word, *What?* if he had a mouth. For some reason, his psionic "voice" wouldn't work. So he raised his arms as if to ask what Statis was doing here.

Statis walked around the mouth, not nearly as grossed out as Jono. He tried to shoot bolts of electricity, but the sparks from his fingertips merely sputtered like dying Fourth of July sparklers.

Then several purple-and-black-clad figures started appearing above them, just below the roof of the mouth. Bevatron, Roulette, Catseye, Tarot, Beef, and the others: the Hellions.

Suddenly, the entire area exploded. The Hellions all cried out in agony as their forms were destroyed. Jono and Walter tried to scream, but couldn't.

And then, hovering in the air before them, was the fearsome, green-haired figure of Trevor Fitzroy, sheathed in armor the way the files said he was that day he came to the Hellfire Club to kill the Hellions.

Fitzroy held out a sword to Jono and Walter that burned with fire.

He held out an enormous electronic firearm bigger than their heads.

He rubbed his hands together and summoned uncounted megahertz of energy that roiled and sputtered in the air.

He raised his arms into the air and laughed a laugh that would topple a city.

Neither Jono nor Walter could remember exactly how it was that Fitzroy killed Emma Frost's former students. It could have been any of these ways, or ways they hadn't thought of. Perhaps they were being tested to see which way of killing them would be the most fun.

Whatever the reason, every horrific threat they could imagine from this murderer threw itself up before them. And every way, they would die.

Emma Frost gave in.

Once, she tumbled through the enormous consciousness of a friend and she was so small in there that she felt as though she were Lucifer falling forever through the depths of Creation. She remembered Dante, the man who had put the story of the fallen angel into words. He was the first man, she realized, to envision and successfully describe a Universe so large that it approached the volume of the real thing. Dante was the first person to begin to understand the scope of Creation. *Perhaps*

Dante was a mutant, her diminishing ego squeaked.

Then what remained of that ego surrendered too, and she was lost again. The last time, she had rescued herself. This time it would fall to her students to rescue her; with her last coherent thought she hoped her mentoring skills had improved since the days when she had mentored the doomed Hellions.

And she fell some more.

Jono and Walter could not speak as Fitzroy pummelled them, but, for some reason—perhaps a by-product of this weird plane where they found themselves, perhaps because of Jono's low-level telepathy that allowed him to "speak" in the real world—they could hear each other's thoughts. So Jono told Walter that this horror was an illusion, but that it was nonetheless real.

Walter thought, *There has to be a way to get word out of this place, wherever we really are right now.*

Keep your strength up, Jono cautioned. *You don't know how much real energy this experience is sucking out of you and you've got little to spare.*

Don't worry about that. I'll have plenty of time to rest. Who can you get in touch with? I can send out a signal.

How?

Walter convulsed as Fitzroy shot him with an energy blast. *This world's so wired for sound and sight I can get any electronic impulse anywhere I want if I just have a pretty good idea of where that destination is.*

Don't send out any signal, Jono urged. *It'll kill you for certain.*

SPIDER WEB

Who else is going to do it? It'll kill everyone else if I don't.

Before Jono could reply, he felt himself being dragged away from Walter. Fitzroy's ever-present cackling receded into the background.

Then Jono felt something odd. He felt he could do something he had never been able to do before. . . .

CHAPTER FIFTEEN
RETURN OF THE PRODIGALS

It was great to be a mutant.

When Skin and Synch stopped for the buffet lunch in Waltham, Everett made the coffee pour itself and Angelo got seconds at the salad bar while he was still sitting in his seat. They were still high on their successful sendup of the Friends of Humanity. Their mood was good as they rolled up the little road to the main entrance of Xavier's School for Gifted Youngsters.

Immediately, they saw that something was wrong.

Half-a-dozen Federal Express packages sat on the road outside the bar that served as a gate to vehicles. Inside the grounds, the first thing they noticed was the big door of the carriage house with all of Sean's car collection—at least those he kept in this country—wide open to the wind and weather. The gazebo was a shambles, its pieces scattered and wet from a rainstorm. It was unlike Emma and Sean to leave the flotsam of an accident or a fight lying around. The two screen doors of the main building flapped open and shut with the breeze.

The headmaster insisted on maintaining this campus the way his family had maintained Cassidy Keep back in Ireland: everything in its place. That dictum held no room for the shards of erupted gazebo or the danger the elements posed to antique automobiles or supposedly urgent overnight shipments sitting by a drainage ditch.

Everett put a finger up to his lips, and Angelo nodded. They rolled the Jeep in neutral to a spot between the carriage house and the river, out of sight of most of the most heavily used areas of the campus.

"Walk lightly, Ange," Everett whispered and they crept out from behind the carriage house and neared the biosphere. On the ground in front of the airlock entrance to the dome, Chamber and Statis lay motionless. Everett almost ran toward them, but Angelo held him back.

"Remember the first lesson," Skin whispered. "Try and figure out what we're seeing first."

"Chamber and the new kid lying on the ground looking dead," Synch whispered back. "Can we go to them now?"

After a moment's thought, Angelo said, "Okay," and they ran for their classmates.

Angelo crouched between both victims, feeling some nameless irritation growing in him about Everett. He felt at Walter's neck for a pulse and discovered it quickly. Everett reached for Jono's neck and hesitated, realizing that there would be no pulse there. Angelo brusquely shoved Everett aside and touched the side of Jono's forehead to find blood coursing through there as well. The bionuclear energy that formed Jono's power also simulated normal involuntary nervous and muscular activity in what remained of his body. He would have a pulse in his forehead, Angelo realized, even if he had died, as long as his chamber still converted ambient matter to energy. That could be several thousand years for all anyone really knew.

"'Smatter with you, man?" Everett asked.

"You're wasting time," said Angelo. "They're both

alive as far as I can tell. Why don't you make yourself useful and get synchronous with the new kid and see if you can figure out anymore, hey?''

Everett scrunched up his lips in an annoyed kind of pout and said, ''I don't know why you're all-of-a-sudden yanking my—''

As he spoke, he put a hand on Jono's upper face. Constellations of energy suddenly tumbled through his physiology, and rolling waves of purposeless anger and pain assaulted his mind and soul. He threw himself back on the ground, rolled over onto his belly and pushed himself up onto his hands and knees in a crouch.

Angelo asked, ''What's wrong? I'm sorry, man.'' He put a hand on Everett's shoulder. ''I didn't mean any—''

Before he could finish, a tiny jolt of bionuclear force poured across the space that separated the two boys. It hurled Angelo upward and over the trees that shielded the compound from the outside world.

Everett regathered his composure and realized what he had done to his friend. He ran through the woods to try to save Angelo.

Angelo, however, was quite capable of saving himself.

His parabolic ascent reached its peak less than twenty feet from the highest leaves of the nearest tree. For a moment, suspended between lift and gravitation, his speed was manageable.

He flung his arms out and downward in two different directions and strands of flesh wrapped themselves around branches below him. Skin suspended himself on the top of the treeline and shifted his weight back and forth to see which of the branches he held was the stabler one. The one he held tightly at the end of his left arm was thin and wobbly; the one he held precariously with his right arm was sturdier. He unravelled the distended skin of his left arm, gathered it up thick in front of his face, and swung down in an arc toward the ground by the straining skin of his right arm.

He extended his legs in front of his fall, shielded his eyes, and hoped his feet made contact with something solid before his face did. Twigs and brush chattered around his ears as Angelo swung downward like a blind king of the apes.

About midway through his teen years, Angelo realized that he did not get hurt. He had lived without any significant fear of physical pain for so long that the source of his usual bravado was a kind of invulnerability. His invulnerability was not that of Penance or the X-Men's Rogue or a solid steel pipe, but rather that of a ball of Silly Putty. Actually, it was better—his remarkable body had developed a conditioned response to pressure. When he got hit, or was about to come in contact with a hard solid object, layers and layers of skin would collect reflexively at the point of impact and cushion the blow.

In midswing, Angelo lost his tenuous grip on the tree limb. He grabbed a stiff birch trunk with his left hand to stop his plummet.

Everett, sprinting through the woods, arrived just in time to see his friend make impact and slide down to the root of the birch tree with his feet wrapped around the narrow trunk that had assaulted him.

"You okay, man?" Everett asked when he made it to where Angelo lay on his back, dazed. "Oh jeez, I'm sorry, Ange. You okay? Say you're okay."

"I'm okay."

"Really?"

"Yeah, I think so." Angelo sat up. "All my fingers are in place. I can feel my toes wiggling. No major bruises."

"Figures," said Everett, contrite. "I'm sorry."

"Of course you're sorry, bro'. I'm sorry, too. But there isn't much to be sorry about. There's something in the air around here and the closer you get to the biosphere the thicker it gets."

"What?" Everett asked with a frown. "What are you talking about?"

"I don't know what, Ev. It's just there, is all. Don't you feel it? You're supposed to be the sensitive one."

"I don't believe my press releases." Everett felt it was safe to smile. "Do you?"

"Not on a bet. Come on. They're in trouble if they're alive, and we're in charge if they're not. Let's get back there."

The demon thought he had now lost the pair that he had overlooked. That would have been unfortunate. The empathetic one had enormous power and control; he would be an even greater weapon than Starsmore. And the other, flexible one, had a delicious spirit.

Unfortunate, but by no means insurmountable, if D'Spayre were to lose these two. No matter in any case. He saw now that their personal protocols made it necessary that they return. He would bring them both home.

At the edge of the woods, Everett and Angelo saw that Jono and Walter had not moved in the past few minutes. But now two figures walked into sight: Paige and Jubilee came out from the biosphere entrance toward the two boys on the ground.

There were signs of life here after all. Everett and Angelo were relieved.

Angelo took a step toward his teammates. Everett grabbed his friend's arm and whispered, "Look."

Paige and Jubilee walked jerkily, almost zombielike. And both Everett and Angelo felt their tempers rise. Something was wrong with them, with everyone at the school.

Angelo crouched behind the rock of some ancient Passamaquoddy farmer's stone wall. "Concentrate on Cambridge," he said.

"What're you talking about?" Everett snapped.

Off in the clearing, Jubilee and Paige moved like cartoon stick figures. Paige took Walter's arms, Jubilee took Jono's.

"We conquered the kingdom to the east today, Ev," Angelo said. "Think about that and blot out the evil in this place."

It made sense to Everett. He felt the tension start to drain from his muscles.

"Let's go out there," Everett said.

"Concentrate," Angelo repeated.

They stepped into the clearing as the girls dragged the unconscious boys toward the entrance of the biosphere, the outer airlock door of which hung open. Inside, it looked like the gates of hell. They both looked away.

"What are you two doing?" Angelo asked the girls.

Neither answered. Neither appeared to hear.

He put a hand on Paige's arm and a physical pain roped his stomach. He fell to his knees. He thought hard about Cambridge.

Everett knew that the same thing would happen to him, so he did not touch Jubilee. He put one hand on Jono's leg, the other on Walter's arm. Neither of the girls noticed, but continued their trek to the outer doorway of the airlock. Everett recoiled as he felt the energy transfer.

He could not bear this time to absorb either unconscious boy's mutant power, but he did become synchronous with them for a moment. He had felt the power pass through him like a battery cable from Walter to Jonothon.

Maybe Jono would be able to do something with it. Something unexpected. Something he himself would have to think of.

Maybe not.

The door closed with their four classmates behind it.

"That was spooky," Everett said.

"Something's watching us," Angelo said.

"I know," Everett said.

"Cambridge," Angelo repeated, almost like a mantra. "Come on back here with me and think about Cambridge."

The two beat a strategic retreat behind the lump in the Earth where the gazebo had previously stood. They looked at each other, breathed heavily, and forced themselves to relax.

CHAPTER SIXTEEN
PACT

Angelo grasped Everett's forearm in a warrior's handshake. Everett grasped back.

"Whatever happens, brother," Angelo said.

Everett repeated, "Whatever happens."

It was a vow as sacred as the Declaration of Independence or the blood brotherhood of Tom Sawyer and Huck Finn.

The pair broke the handshake and faced the open outer airlock door of the biosphere and crouched like sprinters.

Together they said, "Let's go!" They ran to the biosphere at a dead run.

Skin and Synch barrelled through the outer opening of the airlock and collided hard with the inner door, hoping to knock it down. It did not budge a millimeter. Everett almost body-slammed the inner door again when Angelo stopped him.

Skin closed the outer door shut, smirking as if to say, *Why break in when we can go in the normal way?* Everett nodded and turned a knob that swept cool oxygen into the small chamber and quickly reconditioned the air.

Everything worked. This would go fine. They would rescue everyone.

The inner door opened automatically and the pair ran into the biosphere. It smelled like expensive shampoo. They grinned at each other as if to say, *Everything will be fine.* Both took a long breath and considered their next move.

Then it hit them: Nothing would work.

PACT

They knew nothing would work. The ceiling would fall in. The Earth would give way. The air supply would fail. The trees would come alive like the ones on the yellow brick road and strangle and suffocate them in their sleep. Their shoulders they smacked against the door were starting to hurt and they were probably dislocated and their bones would shatter and they'd both get blood poisoning and die. There would be no funeral. Their bodies would rot and they would get sucked up into the ecosystem of the biosphere and spewed off into the air to become part of this horrible place.

Everett Thomas and Angelo Espinoza, hot and high from their adventure in Harvard Square, had strode not ten feet into this big enclosure suffused in gloom before they fell to the ground, huddling against the despondency. Inevitably, their own melancholy smashed them cold and motionless.

Jubilee and Paige came by in their deadened haze, picked them up, brushed them off, and hung them by their wrists from a tree near Jonothon. Then Jubilee and Paige strung one another up, each tugging with her own weight to suspend the other above the ground.

Now the entire student body and faculty of Xavier's School for Gifted Youngsters hung like meat in a freezer.

Some of them like Emma Frost, already tortured for weeks with what she saw to be her failures, did not need to be unconscious in order to disengage from their personalities as the demon required they do. She was battered before being deposited here. Paige Guthrie and

Jubilation Lee, impressionable and eager by nature, were the first other than Frost whom D'Spayre felt comfortable enough to drive on his own. He worked them like puppets.

When Jubilee and Paige had re-hung themselves on their designated trees, D'Spayre strode out from a gathering eddy of space and he saw that it was good.

CHAPTER SEVENTEEN

CURING

D'Spayre was a good innkeeper. Everyone had his or her own private hell where no one else could intrude.

Sean Cassidy was a lord under siege. Sometime last night two daring peasants had scaled the walls and overpowered the drawbridge guard. If the lord of Cassidy Keep ever found a way out of this fix, he would be sure to post more guards at his bedchamber door. But only if he ever found his way out of this.

He lay spread-eagled on a granite slab, tied at ankles and wrists with leather bonds to posts driven deep into the ground below the slab. The sun rose over his head and the crowd of serfs and vassals pressed shoulder to shoulder along the edge of the moat.

"What do you want from me?" Sean demanded in a loud voice that no one seemed to hear. No one seemed to hear anything. "What do you *want* from me?" His voice drowned beneath the din of the hostile crowd. Helpless.

Then Lord Cassidy remembered that this was the day Theresa arrived. She would know what to do. His daughter would be his savior.

A man stood near him, a skinny fellow with sunken cheeks. He wore a tattered black cloth around his shoulders that dragged on the ground but which he sported like a judge's robe.

"It is now time to pass sentence," the man bellowed.

Theresa would come. She would know what to do. Perhaps she was already here.

CURING

"It is the judgment of this court His Lordship is found guilty!"

"Of what—?" Cassidy said in a voice that was drowned in his throat before it could be drowned in the bellowing of his judge and the commotion of the angry peasant mob. Then he pressed on: "Of what am I convicted?"

Where were Theresa and the few most loyal of the manor guard who had accompanied her on her journey? Where was his daughter?

"What gives you the right—?" he sputtered weakly, but he was interrupted by the jeering of the crowd.

"His Lordship," the judge bellowed in a voice that made the granite shudder, "wants to know what gives us the right!"

The resultant laughter and jeering made Lord Cassidy's eardrums bleed.

"It is the further judgment of this court that His Lordship be sentenced to death by slow torture."

Then a figure covered head to toe in black and carrying a jangling sack arose from the crowd and moved to stand beside the granite slab. The figure pulled a curved knife from the sack. Its blade was less than a thumb's length. In a practical sense, it could not kill; its only use was torture. The torturer held the knife blade on Cassidy's throat, pressing the blade firmly against the hollow, but at an angle so it did not break the skin.

As the knife's angle changed and drove up to Cassidy's Adam's apple, His Lordship heard a woman's voice whisper, "Ready?"

Was that the torturer? Was it a female who held this blade to his throat?

A black-gloved hand pulled the hood off the torturer's head and suddenly a hurricane of red hair settled into a mane that framed the leering face of his daughter. Theresa Rourke Cassidy. She was older than he remembered.

The bag full of tempered metal instruments clattered as she leaned forward against it. Another gloved hand tilted and pressed. The torture had just begun, but the despair was already settling in.

Emma was laughing with the Hellions. She could not stop.

"Remembair when I fought wiz Firestar?" Bevatron said in that dense French accent of his.

"Of course," Emma said.

"And you said," Bevatron told her, "you said—do you remembair? You said—"

Together, through chuckling, Bevatron and Emma repeated, " 'Better luck next time!' " Then they both laughed as though they had just caught on to a Jack Benny double-take.

"And ze next time," Bevatron howled, "ze next time I was killed by Trevor Fitzroy!" The French teenager rolled over and over on the carpet laughing, and Emma could not help but join in.

They were in a small living room with six walls and a big fireplace on each wall. There were no doors. Each wall and each blazing fireplace was identical to all five of the others, so she did not know what direction she faced. Somehow, the furniture kept shifting when she was not looking, making it impossible to orient herself.

It was a pleasant room, though, with elegant rugs and comfortable furniture. Catseye curled up on a coffee table in cat form. Jetstream lounged across the davenport. Roulette leaned back in an easy chair flicking the flame of a decorative lighter on and off. Tarot played solitaire with her tarot cards. Beef chewed a cigar, apparently waiting for Roulette's lighter. And there were others. Others whom Emma had known for so short a time she had barely learned their names, let alone focused on their powers and problems enough to send them out into the field.

"'Member when Namorita cleaned my clock?'' Beef cackled. "An' you tol' me—Wha'd you tell me?''

"I said,'' Emma tittered, "I said, 'You better get your act together because you're just a plain boor,' I said.''

"Yeah,'' Beef guffawed. "Real constructive! Then a couple weeks later, Fitzroy dropped me like a sack of meat! Haw! Haw!''

It went on like that. They would each recount their shortcomings and Emma's belittling or inadequate response to them. Then they would laugh, and Emma could not help but laugh too. Then when they were all done, they would go around again. It had been weeks now. Maybe years. Who knew? It was a singular torture: laughing at their pain and deepening hers.

She had never realized before what a welcome release despair could be.

* * *

Penance floated on a cloud, playing a small harp in her lap. It was heavenly.

The strings of the harp broke her fingernails as she tried to strum them. Penance had never had fingernails before, and did not know how to care for them. It was more effort than she expected.

Yvette? a voice asked inside her head.

Who? Penance thought back.

It's Mother, Yvette.

Who?

Your mother. You grew into quite a lovely girl, the voice said.

Mother? There was no mother. Well, certainly there had to have been a mother, but not one she had ever known. There had been the school. And before that there had been Emplate. And before that, nothing. What was this now? Mother?

Of course, Yvette, the mother voice in her head said as Penance trapped two fingers in the coiled metallic strings of the harp. How can a harp be that assertive anyway?

I'm here for you, dear.

Of course there had been a mother. Penance had just not known hers. She had not thought of her, really. Not even the barest glimmer of wonder. Penance had never been the contemplative type: too much else to consider.

She had spent her days with Emplate dodging demons and anticipating the master's needs. At the school, she had mostly lived peacefully in the biosphere or under

CURING

the ground, counting the tendrils in the petals of the tiger lillies, and averaging out the number in her head until she knew the precise probabilities involved in the generations of the tiger lily. Her mind, closed to all—because whom could she trust, after all?—was filled with enormous quantities of botanic and geological information. It filled the cells of her brain as densely as her cells packed in to harden her flesh. She was not sure what she would do with it all on Earth. It was certainly of no use here in eternity.

Don't clutter yourself with concerns like that now, Yvette my darling.

Who are *you?*

Mother of course. I told you that. You need to hit a B-flat with that chord, Yvette. Just a suggestion.

She pulled the sharpening lever down without thinking. Another fingernail cracked off in the harp strings. Penance angrily clapped the back of her hand against the fluff of the cloud on which she sat. Her hand hurt. The cloud was soft but she was softer. How did this happen?

Oh you'll get used to it, dear Yvette.

And where did that name come from anyway? *I'm not Yvette.*

Of course you are.

Who she had always been, as far as she could remember, was Penance—someone who could not be touched. She left destruction just by walking through a place without taking care. Now the air itself burned her face as it whipped by.

GENERATION X

You will get used to it, Yvette dear.

And where was that thick, presumptuous voice in her head coming from? It was driving her mad. This was not heaven. This was despair.

Jubilee was in high school. In first period social studies, someone hit her in the back of the head with a flying paper clip. Dogs consorting in the parking lot out the window attracted the attention of the kids in the fifth row. Mr. Novak the social studies teacher talked in long run-on sentences about the court-packing controversy of the second term of the Franklin Roosevelt administration. The girls in the second row passed notes back and forth about how the teacher's eyes were so deep and did they think his blond hair was real? Pete Succoso in the fourth row grinned and picked his fingernails because he figured they were passing notes about him. Everybody wore a yellow raincoat in class: it was all the rage. Jubilee daydreamed about finding something interesting enough to daydream about; it was all there was to do here.

"Does anyone know the name of President Roosevelt's first appointment to the Supreme Court?" Mr. Novak asked. "Anyone?" He looked around. "Jubilation?"

Oh that's me, she thought. "William Rehnquist?" she said aloud.

"Not bad," Mr. Novak said, "wrong President, wrong judge, right court. Anyone else? Peter, do you know?"

"That would be . . . Jimi Hendrix."

"That would be incorrect."

"Then I don't know."

"That would be correct," Mr. Novak said.

This must be real, Jubilee thought. *I must really be stuck in a high school in Encino with a bunch of kids in yellow raincoats and the world's most boring teachers.*

"FDR's first Supreme Court nomination was Hugo L. Black," Mr. Novak said, "and it was a surprising choice. Black was a Democratic senator from a conservative state who had nonetheless supported the President's New Deal programs all along. . . ."

The girls in the second row passed notes and giggled again. The dogs in the parking lot were starting to howl loudly and the boys in the fifth row suppressed their laughter. Pete the football player preened and the acne-festooned kid in the back of the room pitched another paper clip at Jubilee using a rubber band propulsion system. This one had a note attached, and it hit Jubilee on the back of the ear. She said, "Eep!"

Mr. Novak paused, blank-faced, then looked down from halfway across the room at Jubilee and said, " 'Eep,' Jubilation?"

" 'Eep?' Did I say 'eep?' I meant 'Jeep.' There's that new Jeep with the wider wheel base and the heavy plastic fenders. Out there. See? Where those guys in the fifth row are all looking."

"Plastic fenders?" Mr. Novak said. "Really?"

The note on the paper clip had a locker number and

combination on it and the scrawled message: A SURPRISE FOR YOU! Jubilee looked back at the note's sender, whose acne-covered face smiling from several seats behind her.

I am in hell, Jubilee decided.

Then the principal walked into the room to observe the class. He folded himself into a seat by the back of the room, ingested something from an inhaler, fell asleep, and snored loudly.

Despair, thy name is High School.

Monet had lost her luggage, but that was not the problem. She was in an unfamiliar city, but that was not the problem either. She had no hotel room, no money, no wallet, could not remember her calling card number, and could not find either a pay phone or an automatic teller machine. These were also not the problem.

The problem was that she found herself suddenly aware of what was going to happen in the future, and thus she was out of control.

She was never in control. Monet, however, managed to convince enough people she was, and that made them envious. This was quite enough for her to convince herself she was in control, at least, of her own life. This self-imposed delusion was enough to keep her emotionally afloat.

Knowing the future wiped all that away.

She walked among the people of this odd city. What place was this? Québec? Algiers? Singapore? She did not know, but she knew everything else. As people passed her by, she knew their futures.

CURING

"Take the train tomorrow to your sister's house," she said to a woman in a housecoat and no makeup, "not the plane. Please." The woman was horrified.

Monet walked along the street full of scurrying people. Everybody had a place to go. Everybody had a story. Too many stories. They made her head hurt.

"Excuse me, sir?" she said to a large man with dark eyes and a striped shirt. He stopped, and she said, "You really ought to have a doctor look at that little lump toward the bottom of your back. You know, the one that's irregularly shaped and growing. Any doctor will do. Just have someone—" and then he walked away, not letting her finish.

Is this New Orleans? she wondered. *No, not enough restaurants.*

She saw a man in his late twenties who smiled sweetly. Then a horrific vision of the young man's future slapped across Monet's mind. It was so terrible that she grabbed the door handle of a taxi and motored away.

Johannesburg? No, too many late model cars.

The back of the cab driver's neck was all she could see of him between his shirt collar and his turban, but that was enough. "Would you let me out at the second corner?" she stammered. She paid him, got out of the car and ran halfway down the block before the tanker truck swerved to avoid a pedestrian, collided with an electrical pole, fishtailed into the cab's grille, and blew itself, the cab, and twenty-eight already-doomed citizens including the pedestrian the truck driver had tried to avoid, well into the sky. *What's the use?* Monet wondered.

Calcutta? No, not enough flies.

She covered her face with one hand as she walked and a pair of tattooed arms reached for her wrists. She did not like tattoos very much, but these were different.

"Monet? Are you all right?" Walter Nowland asked.

"Yes," she told him. "Kind of. But we bury you in the third act."

"I know that. Are you sure you're all right?"

"It's a very pleasant funeral. By the river."

"I'm glad to hear that. Monet, you don't look well."

She knew everything about everyone else, but all she knew for herself was despair.

Walter was numb. He tried to make himself care that Monet pulled her arms away from him and scurried with the crowd along the passing parade and vanished. Instead, he just shoved his hands in his pockets and turned down a street and wondered whether he could find a good steak in this town.

Walter sauntered along the back streets of the city, taking in the smells and the vibes. Funny he had never taken a liking to cities before. Always thought there was too much to miss. Too much to worry about. It wasn't worrying him now.

A one-legged vagrant sitting on a corner with a hat in his half-lap asked whether Walter might spare some change. Walter politely demurred.

A man wearing only a medallion on a chain and a

panicky expression shoved past Walter. A large angry woman followed him with a shotgun. Walter stepped out of the way to avoid any gunfire.

Two men were holding a screaming child against the wall of a panel truck. One of the men was shaving the kid's head with a pair of electric shears. Like the other passersby, Walter gave them a wide berth.

None of this seemed to affect him.

Something inside Walter was gently screaming, and it was vaguely uncomfortable that even this silent despair did not seem to be bothering him.

Paige's soft inside was trying to hold on to her hard outside.

Jono was being digested. He was slipping and sliding along the slippery, bumpy surface of a giant tongue.

Once, when Jono was very young, he had maiden aunts who thought he was the cutest little thing. This lasted for about three years—which in little-kid years translates to roughly forever—until his first cousin Wendell was born.

For the first three years of Jono's life—and this was so vivid that he remembered it clearly even now—the moment any of his aunts came to the house, there were lips and tongues all over the place. Large adults would shove their faces so close, he'd see them with kind of a fisheye. There would be puckering lips and these uvulas so close he could practically reach out and touch them anytime someone spoke. With the relatives around, the whole world was a huge mess of saliva and pink things. Too much wet. Too much pink.

For all of his life—and he was sure that poor Wendell suffered the same trauma—Jonothon Starsmore had an aversion to too much wet and pink at the same time. He absolutely could not walk into a Dunkin' Donuts shop. Big lips turned him off. Beaches and public pools gave him the heebie-jeebies. Taste buds—even diagrams like you found in books on anatomy—made his skin crawl. He strangely resented having lost his own facility that he found so unattractive in others: his mouth and sense of taste. The sacrifice made Jono feel even further alienated from humanity than someone in his singular position would have been without such an aversion.

So now here he was, slipping and sliding and wiping off the drool of his worst nightmare. Then a strange thought occurred to Jono. Somehow, he did not trust that any of this was real. Then he wondered whether that really mattered at all. Then he felt something tickling the back of his neck.

Then he remembered he didn't have a neck.

In the Cambridge meeting of the Friends of Humanity, Everett was looking for a way to leave gracefully.

Angelo paced back and forth into and out of the beam of the streetlight in Cambridge, as the Friends of Humanity meeting took place in the lounge of the little apartment building.

*   *   *

CURING

The demon who preyed on these extraordinary young people was feeding them the most sorrowful images he could find buried deep in their ids.

For Sean Cassidy it was the life he might have led and screwed up in an Irish manor house five hundred years ago.

For Jubilation Lee it was also life as it might have been, but for her that was in an excruciatingly tedious high school classroom deep in the wilds of the San Fernando Valley.

For Angelo Espinoza and Everett Thomas it was memories closer to the surface, of experiences of the past few days that brought them both bitter disappointment. But Angelo and Everett had overcome the disappointment and found a measure of vindication in it. Vindication—like love, honor, charity, and the other means to empowerment that had occasionally been his undoing in his dealings with the complex creatures of this world—was a concept for which, even if he nominally held the cure, D'Spayre had no understanding.

"So when the politicians come to you with a ballot initiative," Patrick Harrowhouse said to his assembled followers and in a stage whisper with a conspiratorial glimmer in his eye, "providing special rights for mutants, then you'll recognize the sympathizers by who brings it up and who declares support for it."

Everett gathered up the pieces of his composure, pressed them together into a big ball of initiative, took his hand out of LaWanda's, and said, "Later for you, babe." He slipped out down the hallway.

Angelo sucked in his skin, did a one-eighty under the streetlamp, shook his head so his cheeks rattled and stalked off to the entry of the little apartment building.

The boys met in the hallway of the building.

"You bring the doughnuts?" Angelo asked Everett.

"Doughnuts? What doughnuts?"

"See? That's the reason you're in there and I'm out on the street."

"What are you talking about?" Everett asked.

"It's the proof this all isn't real," Angelo insisted. "You went out to get doughnuts and came back and found me pacing outside. You don't have any recent memory of getting doughnuts, do you?"

"Doughnuts. Oh yeah. I went and got the doughnuts back in Cambridge."

" 'Back in Cambridge.' There you go. That's a memory in the past. Days ago. We're not in Cambridge anymore."

Everett frowned. "I know that."

"Well then where are we?"

"I don't know."

"Look around," said Angelo. "Look deep."

And they did. They looked at the plain yellow walls of the hallway, at the stairwell door painted split-pea-soup green, at the fading color of the single plastic tree in the vestibule. And behind the fake tree was a real willow plant. It faded in and faded out and disappeared.

"Did you see that?"

CURING

"Yeah."

Everett reached a hand toward Angelo's shoulder but couldn't touch it.

"Touch me," Everett ordered Angelo.

"I didn't know you cared."

"Stop screwing around!"

"Just trying to break the mood. I think that's part of the problem."

"The problem," Everett said, "is I can't put a hand on you to set up a synchronicity arc. Maybe you can help."

Angelo could not get his muscles to bring his hand within a foot of Everett. But he could snake a finger out and send it anywhere. His hand stopped as if against a force field inches from his friend's face, but the tendril of skin flowed off him and made contact at Everett's left ear.

"Good, Ange, now wrap it around my neck or something. Get yourself a good grip."

Angelo did that.

"Now look around," Everett said. "Look hard."

They peered at the drab hallway. Then it seemed as though the hallway was covered in a thin, almost imperceptible film of the interior of the biosphere. They looked harder.

"Relax, Ange," Everett said. "It's not like pulling teeth."

Angelo softened his muscles and sharpened his sights. Then the dingy hallway was the translucent image and the biosphere was the clear one. They realized they were not standing on anything. They were both hanging by their arms from trees.

Fifteen feet beyond Everett, Chamber was all wrapped up like a mummy and roped to a big trunk. Past him was Penance enveloped by the trunk of another tree. Statis nearby, his body weakening faster than his mind. And Sean, Emma, and the others.

"You see it?" Everett wanted to know.

"Everything," Angelo said. "The trees, the people, everything."

"See Jono? I think he's closest."

"Yeah."

"Extend the finger around my neck to touch him. Pull it tight if you have to. I need a connection."

Chamber hung lashed against his tree with his face—what there was of it—pressing against the trunk. It was the only way, Everett supposed, to isolate his bionuclear energy. Everett felt Angelo's finger curl and pulse around his neck like a tube going through peristalsis. A wave of flesh moved around his neck and throbbed, then another bulge of flesh started around again in the same direction and flowed forward. The tendril of Angelo's excess epidermis found its way to the tree that held Jono.

Everett felt the tendril of his friend's extended finger tighten around his neck. The finger came to rest on the bandage that masked Chamber's energy from sight. The tip of Angelo's finger was bathed in particles of Jono's enormous life force. Everett reached out to it along the biological bridge that Angelo's distended skin made.

Then Everett discovered something amazing: Cham-

CURING

ber's power allowed him to do things that Jono himself had not even realized he could do yet. There was not a single disability or disadvantage in Chamber's bionuclear cavity for which it did not compensate him a thousandfold if only he stopped brooding and practiced. Flight. Prescience. Long-distance viewing. Remote voice-casting with a real voice. Given time, he could probably create life and travel in time and alter the fabric of reality. He could regenerate his face and give himself a better chin or six heart chambers if he felt like it.

Everett sent a synchronous goose along the biological arc between himself and Chamber; Jono's consciousness gave a start. Then he absorbed a fraction of Chamber's bionuclear power. In that moment, he disintegrated the ropes that held himself and Angelo. He found other ropes somewhere in his mind. When he destroyed them, he heard the sound of someone falling in a heap to the ground.

Angelo was free. The first thing he saw as he retracted his stretched and aching forefinger was Walter, the new kid, tumbling out of a tree. Angelo sprinted toward the fallen boy. Something grabbed his arm in midstride and yanked him back.

It was Everett.

"We freed Chamber but he doesn't know it yet," Everett hissed into Angelo's ear. "Let's get out of here before the fireworks start."

"But the new kid—"

"We've got to live to make it out of here and find out what's taken everyone prisoner and sucked out their brains.'' Everett yanked on Angelo's flexible shoulder. It was ten feet toward the airlock before the rest of him was. "Move it, man!"

Quickly they padded to the exit of the dome as Chamber, not yet even fully conscious, wrestled with wet, sloppy demons in his mind.

CHAPTER EIGHTEEN

FIGHTING BACK

Trooper Mike Brown was driving west along the Massachusetts Turnpike, heading to the Carleton State Police Barracks, when the voice sounded on his radio.

"Mike, you out there?"

The trooper looked at his radio in confusion, perplexed at the uncharacteristic use of clear English on the police band. Every police radio communication is spoken in code to prevent eavesdroppers from having any idea what is being discussed, unless they've memorized entire code books' worth of information.

Still, Mike gamely picked up the handset and replied as he was trained to: "Unit twenty-two check. Trooper Brown. Problem, dispatch?"

"Look, Mike, can the jargon," said the voice, "this is Jono. Do you by any chance have a hole in your schedule just now?"

"I could, kid," Mike said, now a little on the edge.

"Well it's getting a little—" Then the transmission cut off.

Mike considered his options. Jono and his classmates were probably mutants, and mutants meant trouble. A few years back, when Xavier's School was the Massachusetts Academy, the county sheriff's office had gotten a call that the mutant terrorist Magneto planned to attack the school. The sheriff's response was to call in the Avengers.

But Mike couldn't see calling in the Avengers for this one—or even calling in backup, at least not yet.

Then he'd have to explain why, and he couldn't do that without saying that the student body of that ritzy academy in Snow Valley consisted of mutants. That would bring on more trouble than those poor kids really needed.

Besides, he didn't even know what the problem was. For all he knew, Jono wanted him to ferry the Beast around again.

He drove to the other side of the turnpike through the limited-access gap in the island for U-turns, went past the trooper barracks, and headed for the exit to take him to Snow Valley.

An immense voice rang in Jono's head. "A hint of dissension, eh?"

Jono slipped on the tongue of the world and lost contact with his friend the Massachusetts state trooper.

"How did you get free?" the voice demanded.

"I don't know," Jono said truthfully.

Jono stood in two places: on a slippery, seemingly organic surface and, at the same time, in the biosphere. It wasn't as though they phased back and forth, actually. Rather, he was in both places at once, the interior of the biosphere existing as a kind of hazy indistinct backdrop behind the gauze curtain of this strange place.

Is it a place at all? Jono wondered, then dismissed the thought. He had no stomach—so to speak—for philosophical musings.

"I require that resistance be eliminated," the voice

said. Jono held his hands to his ears out of reflex, but it brought no relief. The sound came, not through his ears, but through his body, rattling his soul.

And Jono felt something on his shoulder—something like a hand, only bigger. He wheeled around and saw, for the first time, the face of D'Spayre—

—but the face belonged to Jonothon Starsmore.

"Where are you going, Michael Brown?" the radio demanded.

For the second time in five minutes, a voice came over the radio in Mike's unit that did not belong to the dispatcher and spoke in plain English. But this time, the voice was not Jono's. It carried a deeper timbre, and filled Mike with a terrible sense of dread.

"Greetings and welcome to my radio," Mike said, "now get out of town." He flipped the device off, not wanting to hear the voice anymore.

"You wouldn't be thinking of coming out here, would you, Mike?"

He looked again. Yes, the radio was indeed off. But the voice would not go away.

"Would you, Mike?" it asked again.

Uh-oh, Mike Brown thought, and hit ninety as he approached the exit for Snow Valley.

Chamber unloaded his midsection into the face that D'Spayre wore, burning his own features off them. The face had a lower half, the face that Jono had worn years ago before his power took him over and made him a freak.

As his complete face melted away, Jono felt a pang of loss. The teen-rock-star face had earned him screams and girls' fainting spells and the occasional chase through hotel hallways, but still he blew it away.

The demon stood his ground, rotated his head on his thick neck, sucking it all in as the handsome younger Jono, and twisted the ends of his demon mouth upward into a profane smile.

For a moment, Jono saw the familiar surroundings of the biosphere. The triangular and hexagonal support struts of the wall enclosed the lush forest. From a tree beyond the clustered fronds of a dense date palm, Paige's legs dangled. Sprinklers, controlled by timers, spritzed water selectively through this artificial rain forest. But he did not feel the moisture although it wafted through and around him. He saw all these things through the slimy, dolorous reality that this demon had constructed over it, pasted like wallpaper over his perceptions.

Jonothon Starsmore had heard of D'Spayre, and knew how he had been bested before: against a bright burst of optimism this creature would go down. But Jono had no need for any such bravado. He did not feel the rush that some others felt from wielding their talents, and he had little use for those who enjoyed such things. He was a guy without a face, a throat, a heart, lungs, or anything else down to his thighs. He was held together by the memory of a body projected onto a chamber of roiling unimaginable power. He hated his life and he lived with it anyway.

The only surcease he owned was the knowledge that he could blow it all away if he chose with a rogue burst of psionic power. How could a blast of despair rolling across this nasty forsaken place like a nuclear heat wave do anything to make what passed for his life worse than this? He laughed at D'Spayre. The dour Scot generally did not laugh out loud, especially since he had to go to the trouble to simulate laughter with his psionic voice. But he laughed inwardly, the way a dying man might laugh.

It did not matter where he was, even if he was in the slime-drenched cavern of D'Spayre's twisted reality. He was already trapped inside himself. He was unlike anyone else, human, mutant, or freak. He had no pride in himself, but no sorrow either. And that made him the perfect opponent to D'Spayre.

Chamber would not surrender to despair in the face of the failure of his power. The demon only huffed larger and stronger with Chamber's failure. The villain still moved closer. Jono felt no despair because it was an emotion he had long ago dismissed.

Until now. He looked down and saw that the energy of his midsection chamber was gone. It had petered out so profoundly that there was not even enough of it to hold the rest of him together.

What was left of Jonothon Starsmore's ''self'' was

simply that portion of his head from his nose to his scalp.

It took forever for him to tumble to the ground.

Walter groggily lay under the hefty branches of an elm, with no idea how he got into the biosphere. He saw a scuffle with Chamber caught up in it. Every time Chamber came into view, sliding into and out of Walter's line of sight as he raced around the dome, he seemed to pop in and out of existence, like a strobe light that shined on him and nothing else. Statis could not figure out what he was fighting, or why.

Then he heard a white pounding in his head that sounded like noise but did not feel like it. Lights flashed from the directions in which Jono ran, jumped, or rode his own heat waves. But unlike the steady flashes you normally saw from Jono, the lights were flickering bands of brightness punctuating the skylit incandescence in the biosphere. Jono's power, like Jono himself, seemed to be flickering in and out of reality. And the ground rattled when he shifted in and out of phase—on a short delay, the way a clap of thunder follows a bolt of lightning.

So where did he go when he wasn't here?

Statis moved toward the noise. He saw Jono for a moment beyond the leaves of a thin tree, but then he vanished. Walter went to the spot and saw nothing, but felt an immense static charge in the air.

Walter walked through the airlock of the biosphere

and found himself in the chill, brisk air of a New England forest. Although he was bone-tired, having exerted himself to an unreasonable degree, he suddenly felt great. He was sick and dying, but suddenly that was all right. He wondered if there was something wrong with that.

"Hey! Walter!" somebody called from off to the side of the biosphere. Someone behind him gave him a tap on the shoulder.

Walter looked at his shoulder and was alarmed to see the tip of a finger, which then snapped back to the hand it had come from—about twelve or fifteen feet away.

"Walter, you all right, man?" the thin, ashen-faced kid said as he trotted to Walter's side. The walls of the biosphere clattered with the conflict inside and the ground rumbled below him. Skin stumbled as he ran.

"Oh. Angelo, right?"

"Yeah."

"I'm fine. What's going on?"

"Everett and I sprung you from inside that hellhole. Glad you made it out. He's up in Sean's office trying to find out the name of this nut case that's trying to take down the school."

"D'Spayre," Walter said. "He's called D'Spayre. Heard of him?"

"No, but that doesn't mean anything. Let's go tell Synch and see if anyone's told the database how to take him down."

FIGHTING BACK

*   *   *

Earthquakes can't be felt in a moving car unless they are really big, the kind that knock down bridges. Mike Brown did not notice the ground rattling until he stopped his car at the gate leading into Xavier's School, and thought he felt the engine knocking. He made a note to chew out the guy in the motor pool for watering the high-octane gas with regular until he put a foot on the ground and noticed the vibrations running up his calf. A collection of Federal Express boxes rattled off the edge of the road and gradually settled in the runoff gully covered with traces of remnant snow.

Taking pity on the tumbling boxes, Mike gathered them up and piled them in the trunk of his unit. Then he grabbed the radio receiver. "Unit twenty-two to Dispatch."

"Dispatch," the radio said. "Come in unit twenty-two. Over."

The dispatcher's voice sounded unusually calm for someone within throwing distance of an earthquake. True, Mike had never been in an earthquake before, but this sure felt like one.

"Do we have any specifications yet on the earthquake in progress? Over."

A pause.

"Earthquake?" Dispatch asked. "Over."

"Reporting an earthquake in Snow Valley. Please contact United States Geological Survey in Colorado. Trooper Brown out."

"Colorado?" the radio said. "Earthquake? There are

no earthquakes in Massachusetts. Mike, are you all right?"

But Mike Brown was now running toward the biosphere.

Mutants meant trouble.

He was conscious. There was no reason Chamber should be alive, let alone conscious, but here he was, lying on the slimy, sticky surface of one of the top ten visions of hell. Over him stood the slime-master himself, D'Spayre.

"Oh, so tasty," the demon said.

This place seemed more and more like some monster's foul gullet. Jono's face lay at a sideways angle to the surface where soft little buds began to rise and contract. In one direction was a tunnel. From the opposite direction, little points of light peeped through the darkness, glowing on and off in irregular patterns.

D'Spayre crouched over Chamber's discarded legs, which rode the soft surface, spiky buds bobbing up and down underneath them. D'Spayre lifted one of Jono's legs, ran it under his face, closing his eyes lightly and drinking it in as if it were a Havana cigar.

Then the creature flung the leg toward the maw. It flew in an irregular spiral like a knuckleball. A uvula-shaped object snapped down and caught it like a frog snatching a fly out of the air. The leg rolled into the appendage for a moment, then tumbled backward into the darkness.

D'Spayre knelt down to look into the eyes and half-face that remained of Jonothon Starsmore. For a moment, Jono understood the way a bird must feel when a python catches its eye and freezes it in place before striking. Then Jono shook off the hypnotic gaze.

He had no mouth and he needed to scream.

Walter felt good and rather energetic as Skin helped him, hobbling with the Legacy Virus despite his effusive mood, toward the back door of the main school building.

"You okay?" Angelo asked.

"Fine, fine," Walter said, happily fighting both his rubbery legs and the rumbling Earth to keep his footing. "Fine as kine."

"Fine as what?"

"Kine."

Angelo frowned. "What's that?"

"Cattle. Kine. I think it's an Irish thing."

"Oh," Angelo said. As Walter leaned on his shoulder, he hooked open the screen door with his foot and pulled it open with his free arm.

"Or maybe it's a rancher thing."

"Whatever," said Angelo as he balanced precariously on his remaining leg. "The infirmary's right in here if you want to—"

"Somebody's coming," Walter said. He felt an approaching electrical aura from the far side of the building before Angelo could hear the tight pattern of running against the quaking ground. Still leaning on Angelo, Walter unloaded a long stream of static charges, which hung on the air like a fence from the far edge of the building to about twenty yards beyond.

Trooper Mike Brown came lumbering around the corner, face-first into the charged air. He got caught in it, seeming to hang in the air like Greg Louganis at the top of the arc of a dive.

The charge in the air dissipated, and the big trooper fell to the ground with a bloody scrape on his nose.

Walter fell backward onto his bony backside. "I guess that wasn't such a good idea. Are you all right, Officer?" he called to Trooper Brown.

The cop slowly rolled himself onto his back and tasted the blood dripping into the corner of his lips and onto his charcoal gray, pleated uniform trousers. "Jono called me. I think. Are you two what passes for security in this place?"

"No sir," Angelo said. "Usually the headmaster takes care of that, but he's a prisoner of a super-villain right now."

"Then I probably shouldn't replace these pants just yet, is that what you're saying?"

Mike got to his feet and gently helped Walter up by the waist. "So tell me, kids," he asked, "where's the headmaster and this super-villain?"

Before either could answer, the ground shook like a salt shaker. A deep rumbling came from the side of the building around which Mike had come running. Angelo ran to the corner of the building. Everett slid open the window of Sean's office and leaned out to see what was going on. Mike scooped up Walter in both arms and slid along the wall with him so they would not fall as the ground shook.

All four saw a big hexagonal section burst straight up from the top of the biosphere. All four shielded their eyes when the pillar of fire followed it.

CHAPTER NINETEEN

THE FORMER BIOSPHERE

Now that the prey was driven into an insane rage, the demon was able to feed permanently, increasing his power. Once, D'Spayre had taken unto himself the fury of a single man—a tyrant who had seduced a nation and murdered millions and had felt exultation rather than remorse. The taste of the man's madness had made D'Spayre larger, stronger, given him a perceptible rush for decades that was so strong he had hibernated for most of that time, assimilating the power. He thirsted for more.

These creatures were delicious. They had brains quite large enough and adaptable enough to overcome any emotional or instinctive response, but they were in a peculiar stage of development where they were either disinclined or unable to make primarily intellectual decisions. From their enslaved masses to their most powerful leaders, they all thought with their endocrine systems rather than their minds. And oh, those minds: so powerful in potential, so aware, so practiced at enduring.

Humans seemed to prefer disaster to serenity, they solicited it so. What a fine symbiotic relationship D'Spayre could foster when he took the essence of Starsmore to himself. He was the natural leader and most powerful of these young ones—who could easily rule this delectable planet with the proper balance of ambition and artifice. They—and even the older ones who oversaw this compound, Frost and Cassidy—would follow this Starsmore to the ends of creation. The remainder of the world would wash up in their wake out of ignorance.

There were others like D'Spayre in the universe. There were not many; such as this demon do not reproduce casually. But this warren of beleaguered souls—so subject to fear, so adaptable to suffering, so inclined to exploitation—this Earth, was D'Spayre's quiet little secret from them. To rule this world was to feed forever.

Oh, what a luscious planet.

Chamber's belly was itching. It happened sometimes—a phantom pain also common to amputees—so that didn't bother him. But his toes itched as well. Not a phantom pain, he knew those. This was a genuine itch.

But his toes, along with the rest of his body from the lower end of his chamber downward, had been unceremoniously tossed aside by D'Spayre. So how could they itch?

Answer: Jono's brain stem had not been disconnected from the rest of what passed for his body. It was still rooted firmly in a pool of bionuclear psionic soup no matter what lies this inter-dimensional illusionist planted in his brain.

So, he thought, *if I'm whole and not lying here in pieces on a great sucking tongue, the next logical step is to blow the dump's doors off.*

So he did.

To his surprise and delight, the next thing Jonothon saw was the flash of his bionuclear blast. Then Jono saw the demon's mouth turn to shards of demon jaw. The concussion of Jono's blast hurled the creature up above his head.

Jono's body returned to normal, for him. The lower half of his head was composed of that bionuclear soup again, but he was used to that. His legs were under his torso where they belonged, as was the rest of him. The grisly gullet faded off Jono's world like strips of crepe paper the day after Halloween. He was in the biosphere. He had never left it.

A shock wave lifted D'Spayre away from him. In the path of that expanding shock wave, Paige, Monet, Emma, Sean, Penance, and Jubilee hung from trees.

Oh hell, he thought.

He looked up at the roof of the biosphere in that instant that D'Spayre was riding, in pieces, the psionic flume. He realized that the explosion carrying the demon would blow the biosphere to pieces. But first it would curve against the interlocking surfaces of the structure, ricochet in all directions, and thus decimate everything and everyone inside the dome. Then it would blow open a panel somewhere in the surface and fling its energy off into the local environment.

His problems, then, were twofold. First, the contents of the interior of the biosphere would be decimated, including his teachers, his classmates, and himself. Secondly, this nuclear energy would then be released into a local environment that included two small mountain ranges, several river valleys, hundreds of contained and interlocking ecosystems, an extensive groundwater supply, a small but heavily populated state, and the eastern segment of a large and even more heavily populated one.

This was unacceptable. That was why, in that instant before the explosion, Chamber decided that he was going to die.

From the deepest recess of his soul, Jonothon Starsmore visualized his power. In his mind, he saw a beam of contained and controlled bionuclear energy shooting up from his gut to the topmost hexagon of the biosphere structure. It would form a tube of energy surrounding the wild burst that was vaporizing the demon D'Spayre and, unchecked, would flatten the Berkshire Hills.

Maybe Jono could make this vision a reality, but who knew how the blast he gave D'Spayre had damaged him? What would be left of him now?

He assumed there would be nothing.

There was only one way to find out.

The power poured out of him, and it came in the shape, not of a cylinder, but of a funnel. It was an enormous fusion firebreak, scooping upward and containing everything Jono had unleashed, and all the demons he had contained. Before it burst through the walls of the biosphere, the top end narrowed so that it was indeed a cylinder. The piston of force propelled forward.

Jono realized that he had not unleashed this power— rather, he *was* this power. His being was scooped up in the wild ride of nuclear force. It was Jono himself who rode upward crashing through the topmost hexagon of the dome and, for all his restraint, vaporizing it and everything it touched.

The light was blinding, the noise, disorienting. He

knew nonetheless where he was and what he was doing, and despite his power, he was burning himself.

On the edge of space, Chamber stopped his ascent. The chaotic energy that had been the demon D'Spayre spewed out of the cylinder of containment and into the vast nothingness, off the blunt northern peak of the solar system. Every atom, every quark that had once been the corporeal form of D'Spayre would occupy a separate parsec of the void. All the king's horses and all the king's men would find it easier to reassemble a beam of light into a tungsten filament than to put this demon back together again.

Everett vaulted off the windowsill of Sean's office, tucked and rolled as he hit the ground, and came up in a run toward the erupting biosphere.

Angelo took off as soon as he heard the sound, not missing a beat as Everett landed running not three steps in front of him.

Trooper Brown gently set Walter down against the wall of the building by a corner to shield him from the blast, and he lit out, unholstering his weapon as he did so.

Walter, however, would not be left out of action so easily. Though unable to stand, he could still fire a charge. An electrostatic arc shot from Walter's fingers, enveloping the cop, Skin, and Synch. It would not keep out everything, but it would effectively discourage the passage of high-level nuclear particles.

But with the electric ''sac'' he covered Everett with,

he caught the slightest frisson of energy returned along the electrostatic arc: Everett's wave of synchronicity.

The interlocking frame of the structure conducted the fire of the nuclear blast that flew cleanly out the topmost hexagonal panel of the biosphere. What remained first glowed red, then white, then darkened to black, then sagged, then was ash. Hundreds of delicate forms of plant life were suddenly introduced to the vagaries of the elements in a New England springtime.

The wave of heat flew up like a comet to the edge of space. Emma, Sean, Jubilee, Paige, Penance, and Monet were caught in its tail. They all became entangled in the trees—except for Sean and Jubilee, who shot past the treeline and catapulted into the air.

Sean came to forty feet above the ground and twisted himself toward the spinning, yellow-coated figure of Jubilee. He managed to grab her by an ankle twenty feet over the approaching earth, yanked her close to him as he flung his head at a crazy angle and let out a Banshee roar. With that, he gained control of his flight, and was able to guide himself and his student to the ground.

Mike Brown found Emma draped over a tree limb by her waist, as if left as bait for wild animals. He clapped his gun back in its holster, lifted her off the branch, and flung her fireman-style over a shoulder.

Everett approached Penance, who seemed embedded in the trunk of a nearby tree. Everett allowed himself to be drawn into her gravitational pull and touched her on the forehead, replicating her density. She woke at his touch, stepped out from the tree, and spun once on her heel. She dropped into the ground below Everett's feet. He promised himself to try that sometime.

He then shot twin bolts of Statis's electrostatic force at Paige and Monet, now dangling by their elbows from high limbs. Those branches cracked as if struck by lightning. The power surprised Synch as he used it. He rolled forward as the two girls fell. It was all he could do to shed Penance's dangerous density and strength as Paige came down hard on his shoulders. The ground and undergrowth he fell on was still hot from the explosion.

Monet's reflexes fell into place as she woke up, and she floated down to the ground softly as a leaf. "What?" she asked Everett groggily.

"We're fine now," Everett said, getting up from under Paige and then lifting her in both arms. Monet scooped them both up and flew them all out of the newly formed hot zone. They all felt like they were waking from a nightmare.

Sean landed in a depression of lawn far from the buildings and, holding Jubilee around the shoulder, walked her back to where the group was reassembling. All of them were waking up, returning to consciousnesses and their accustomed composures. Walter stumbled out to the lawn where everyone gathered so he could see what was left of the biosphere.

There was nothing left of the biosphere, other than a charred circle a foot or two thick around the arcane plant life that it used to contain. Penance surfaced near where the biosphere had stood and Sean saw her as he tried to account for everyone.

Monet disdainfully fingered a shred of her sleeve, or what was left of it. Other than Mike's trooper uniform, everyone's clothing was in tatters.

"I've got to order more clothes right away," Sean said almost to himself. Then he remembered the order he had placed over the internet a week or so or maybe a century ago. "Anybody seen any FedEx packages?"

"They're in my trunk," Mike said. "What I want to know is, where's Jono? He called me on my radio. That's why I came. Where is he?"

"Jonothon spoke on your radio?" Sean asked. "He's never done that before."

"Well, he did it about fifteen minutes ago," the cop said.

A heavenly light poured down from the sky. It did not come from the sun, which hung low in the sky.

The light became tendrils that wrapped around one another like the patterns on the outermost edges of the rings of Saturn. It fell and collected like a pile of sifted sand. It formed into a swirl of visible photons, then a tangle of flying cells, then a mesh of tiny interconnected tubes like the pattern of a human capillary system.

The light became flesh.

And the flesh became Jonothon Starsmore.

For a moment, Jono stood on the lawn, together and whole as he might have been had he grown to this age with a face and a torso. He faded as the others stood and watched, amazed, somehow feeling that this was to be expected of this extraordinary young man.

And Jono stood, naked and whole, glowing like the light he had been moments ago. He held out a hand to Paige, who reached back. Unfortunately, before she could touch him, his midsection burst into a blinding light.

The area from his groin to his upper lip again roared with a furnace of bionuclear power. Chamber was back. Only Everett, summoning traces of an indefinable power, could look at him full-on.

"Maybe now would be a good time to get those packages out of my car," Trooper Mike Brown said, and jogged toward the closed gate.

CHAPTER TWENTY

COMING TRUE

In the spring and half-summer Walter Nowland spent as a member of the student body at Xavier's School, he helped flummox the plans of an inter-dimensional demon, he helped rebuild the biosphere, and he found the closest friends he would know in his brief sixteen years. He took classes in trigonometry from Sean Cassidy and on business writing from Emma Frost. And he got to be on hand for several other interesting events.

Monet's evil brother, Emplate, posing as a long-lost cousin from Algeria who wanted Monet to return home to her father's estate, nearly kidnapped both Monet and Penance.

Everett found himself in a brawl with a collection of neo-Nazis from Vermont and, in the course of sending them on their way, learned how to develop a synchro-nous aura with certain mutant strains of plants—notably a spiny quill-spraying little beastie that grew in the bio-sphere. He could not get the knack of disassembling and levitating inanimate objects again, though, and he sus-pected that some secret mutant in the crowd back at Harvard Square owned that power and he was just bor-rowing it at the time.

Meanwhile, Walter was on and off intravenous feed-ing and painkillers and the occasional tank of oxygen, and to his surprise managed to pass the time fairly com-fortably. In the last days of his life, he had the time of his life.

* * *

COMING TRUE

The new biosphere was completed by the middle of the summer, and it looked better than it had before. One morning in early August, with great ceremony and ritual, Chamber and Husk carried Statis each with a hand under his thigh and another on his lower back, to turn the key that activated the filtration system and the hydraulic pump that maintained the vacuum in the airlock. Paige had to help him get the key in the hole, but Walter turned it himself. A slow hissing noise sounded for four or five seconds as the pump sucked the air out of the airlock. The ground rumbled as the filtration system kicked in. Everyone took a deep breath and looked at the headmaster.

In a voice rich with resonance, whose vibrations the students could feel down to their feet, Banshee bellowed: ''Yes!''

''You know,'' Walter said with a smile, ''sometimes wishes do come true.''

Everyone else—Emma, Jubilee, Skin, M, Penance, and Synch—talked with Walter as Paige and Jono placed him gently back on the air mattress they had put out for him against a tree near the biosphere all throughout its reconstruction. Walter was thinner than he had ever been before, and weaker. Sean called the Beast, ostensibly to check the ecological integrity of the new biosphere. In truth, the headmaster wanted Dr. McCoy nearby for Walter.

As Sean pocketed his cell phone, Walter fell unconscious.

*   *   *

After bringing Walter to the infirmary to await Hank McCoy's arrival, the students wandered the grounds by themselves, piecing together their thoughts. Jono walked to the Mad River. The day was beautiful.

Lost in thought, he did not notice Paige sitting in the crook of the three main branches of a large sugar maple over his head. "What do you make of it, Jono?" she asked.

Chamber jumped, spun, and looked up at the voice. "I thought I was alone here," he said, squinting and putting an arm up against the sun.

Paige laughed and swung down from her perch.

Jono asked, "What do I think about what?"

"Losing Walter."

"I never met a guy who was less afraid of dying."

Paige joined Jono in his river-side walk. He made no objection. They strolled together for a little distance up the bank of the river that Paige so loved. It was hardly mad. Here in the dog days of summer, it was barely a trickle.

"What was the line?" she asked. "When a friend dies, you lose a friend, but when you die you lose all your friends."

"Jack Lemmon," Jono said.

"Really? He's pretty healthy, isn't he?"

"Yeah, but he played a guy who was dying in a movie called *Tribute*. He was this very self-indulgent superannuated teenager. Not much like Walter."

"So we're losing a friend," Paige said with a touch of sadness.

"He doesn't look at it that way. Last week he was talking about coming back to haunt us. He's thinking of setting up housekeeping at the new gazebo."

"Better be careful," Paige said. "Sean will send his parents a tuition bill."

"Oh don't worry about Walter's ghost," Jono dead-panned. "He's on scholarship."

Paige tried to remember the last time she heard Jonothon say something in fun. When she could not recall one, she decided not to laugh for fear of scaring him away. She smiled instead.

Paige has a great smile, Jono decided. *Maybe I should crack a joke more often.*

"You're actually sounding optimistic, my little bag-pipe," she said after a moment.

"First time for everything, my little pachyderm," he answered.

"It's kinda weird, since your pessimism beat D'Spayre. Can't we count on that anymore?"

He thought. "Not pessimism," he said, "skepticism. And it's still healthy."

By the time the Beast made it to the campus, there was not much left of Walter. He had drifted in and out of consciousness. He must have known on an instinctive level that it was time to let go. There was little Hank could do.

"Should I put him on a morphine drip?" Emma suggested, readying the IV stand.

"No," McCoy told her. "There's no indication that he's in pain. He's past that."

Emma listened to Walter's mind to confirm the prognosis.

Walter spoke shakily. "Hiram?" He reached to a point in space next to the Beast.

"Who's Hiram?" the doctor asked Emma.

She shrugged, but she heard a voice that was not Walter's in the boy's mind. *Think I'd let you leave here without me, little scalawag?*

"It's the first sign of incoherence I've observed," McCoy noted.

As he spoke, a visible thin electrical arc flashed from Walter's crown to his toes under the sheets. A moment later the lights in the room dimmed, browned out, and then flashed brighter than before. The electricity in the infirmary and in this wing of the building stopped short. Emma quickly went to the window to open the shade, navigating the darkened room with telepathic ease.

Just as Emma found the shade, and before she let its sliver of light in, she heard the Beast say: "Time of death, sixteen-hundred-and-four hours."

With the light that Dr. McCoy did not need, Emma looked up at the clock on the wall over the infirmary door. Indeed, it had stopped at four minutes after four.

After a minute, Emma said, "I'll call his parents."

"What I will remember about Walter Nowland," Emma said, "was that he taught me responsibility has two edges."

COMING TRUE

They stood—the students, the teachers, the Beast, the Massachusetts state trooper and his wife, and Walter's parents, sister, and four brothers from Nebraska whom Sean had flown in—in a little clearing in the forest by the Mad River. Walter's coffin sat suspended over a deep rectangular hole in the glade. It was not as though the place was a graveyard, but scattered all along the river were unobtrusive little memorial stones to mark the burial places of eight or ten lost heroes—like the wooden markers you would see along the Cumberland Trail or the Santa Fe Trail years ago, to mark the resting spots of travelers or mail carriers or adventurers who fell along the way.

"I will remember," Emma went on, "that each of us must walk our own path, most of us blindly, and that whatever guidance we can give one another when those paths cross is a bonus. It's a valuable lesson for a student to give a teacher."

Then they went around the group remembering Walter. Everett spoke about the way he perked up the wilting potted ferns in the dorm building with a little jolt of static electricity to their main root stems. Paige recalled how the white rose tattooed on his arm wiggled when he passed a plate across the dinner table. Jubilee thanked him for his account of his public high school back in Nebraska, and for letting her know she shouldn't feel too sorry for the kids who had to go to them. Sean remembered him for teaching him that everyone is worth listening to.

His oldest brother, Harley Jr., told a story of how,

when Walter was eleven, he burned a big circular pattern in a flat corner of the north cattle pasture. Walter had suppressed his laughs while reporters from newspapers in four counties tried to prove or disprove that alien visitors had landed there to rustle cattle on their way home to Betelgeuse. Harley Sr., hearing the story, feigned surprise and disappointment, saying he would never be a party to such a hoax, and the old man's performance managed to turn his wife's tears into reluctant but inevitable laughter.

Jono was the last to speak. "What I'll remember about Walter, is that he was a guy who always knew just where he was going." He rapped a fist lightly on the coffin and looked up into the sky.

Around the little grove in the woods by the Mad River everyone else looked up too.

When **SCOTT LOBDELL** isn't writing the monthly comics *Uncanny X-Men*, *X-Men*, *Iron Man*, and *Generation X* (which he co-created with Chris Bachalo and has written since its inception in 1994), or playing favorite uncle to his twenty nieces and nephews, he's enjoying his perpetual honeymoon with the Lovely Laura.

ELLIOT S! MAGGIN has written nearly 500 comic book stories and graphic novels, including a fifteen-year period as principal writer of *Superman*, as well as teleplays and screenplays. He is the author of the best-selling Superman novels *Last Son of Krypton* and *Miracle Monday*. He has also designed computer games, written extensive software documentation, written speeches for several political and entertainment figures, and taught English and journalism at three colleges. He has been a ski bum, raised thoroughbred horses, and was once a Democratic candidate for Congress. Maggin lives in the San Fernando Valley with his wife, their two children, an enormous Labrador retriever, and enough data processing power to operate a small, fairly backward country.

TOM GRUMMETT started doing commercial illustration while working for the Saksatoon Board of Education's printing department. His first comics work appeared in the 1980 *Captain Canuck Summer Special*, and he went on to work on *The Privateers* and *The Shadowalker Chronicles*. In 1989, he started doing fill-in work for DC Comics, including issues of *Animal Man*, *Secret Origins*, *Action Comics*, and *Wonder Woman*. He has served as the regular penciller on *The New Titans*, *The Adventures of Superman*, *Robin*, *Superboy*, and, for Marvel, *Generation X*. Tom presently lives in Saksatoon, Saskatchewan, Canada, with his wife, Nancy, and their two children.

DOUG HAZLEWOOD has been inking professionally since 1985. After winning the inking category of the "Official Marvel Try-Out Contest" in 1986, he plunged into comic books full time. He has enjoyed stints on the critically acclaimed *Animal Man* and was a part of the death and resurrection of Superman on *Adventures of Superman*. Doug currently is the inker on *Superboy* for DC Comics. A native Texan, he lives in Victoria, Texas, with his wife and two children.